These Golden Years

A COLLECTION OF SHORT STORIES

SARA R. TURNQUIST

If you would like to stay up-to-date on this and other series from Sara and receive a free ebook, sign up for her newsletter:

https://saraturnquist.com/list

For Aiden, my son,
Your laughter is infectious.

January

ALL THAT GLITTERS IS NOT GOLD

Owen Miller, whom most called "Uncle Owen," watched his bride of three years as she moved about the kitchen. Never did he tire of marveling at the woman he had wed. She was smart, efficient, pretty... and not to mention, the best cook this side of the Rio Grande.

Even now, she bustled about, here and there, making breakfast preparations. Not for the first time, he thought perhaps he should help. But as he moved to stand, he remembered the last time he'd had such a thought...and acted on it. That was a day that would forever be in his mind for as long as they both should live. He hadn't known Dorothy's words could turn so sharp.

Bottom line—he was not to be in her kitchen.

She wasn't wrong in her decision. He had been underfoot and in the way, despite his best intentions. So now, he satisfied himself watching from his seat at the dining table. If she needed him, she'd ask. Wouldn't she?

The aroma wafting from the kitchen was wonderful, as usual. But Dorothy seemed rather quiet this morning. It was she who usually chatted on during these stretches. It wasn't in his nature to prattle. Should he, however, engage her in conversation? Just this once?

Who knew? Maybe she waited on him to take an interest. Women could be strange like that.

"Smells good." It was the only thing he could think to say. Seemed reasonable.

"Um hmm," came her short reply. Followed by the clanging of a plate as she spooned eggs onto it.

"I reckon I ain't had vittles this good in all my life."

She had turned and stepped toward him but halted. "All your life, eh? What about all those meals I made at the Miller Ranch over the last decade?"

Oops. Owen swallowed. "I mean, besides those."

One of her eyebrows rose. "So, this is the best eating you've had ever except for the last so many years of breakfasts, lunches, and dinners. That's what you're saying?"

"Aw, shucks, I'm just trying to say you're the best cook I've had the pleasure to eat after."

Her eyes narrowed. "I see."

What now? What had he said? What could he say to fix it?

"Well, eat up." She fairly dropped the plate in front of him. Then moved off toward the stove.

Had he vexed her so? Or was this one of her moods? He still couldn't figure it all out. Picking up his fork, he offered her a grin. "Smells even better up close."

"That so?" She glanced over her shoulder. "Owen Miller, are you starting without me? Without saying grace?"

He paused, forkful of eggs midair. "Course not. I was just cooling off my first bite." Then he blew lightly on the yellow fluff.

"You saying I didn't serve it just right?" Now she faced him, her hands on her hips.

"Goodness, no." He slammed his fork to the plate. The eggs bounced off onto the table. "I just meant that—"

"I know what you meant," she said, dishing herself some eggs. "And I can't say that I appreciate it very much."

What had happened here? How had his simple compliment gone so wrong? It was certain—there was something up her crawl. But what?

He watched her as she finished putting food on her plate and returned to the table. She kicked her chair back with a foot and landed in the seat. "Aren't you gonna return grace?" The words were spoken without looking at him. Something was very wrong here.

"Sure, Dorothy, I'll say thanks for—"

She folded her hands and jerked her chin heavenward. "To Him. Not me."

Owen was glad she couldn't see the slight tremble in his hands before he clasped them. "Dear Lord..."

She let out a long, rather heavy exhale.

It took only a moment for him to gather his wits again. "We thank You for this food and the provision of my lovely wife, whose hands prepared it."

He peeked in her direction to see her grimace.

Then he continued. "Please bless her real good and help me be a fitting husband."

He paused again.

Her breathing was louder than he'd like. Was it impatience? Perhaps that was all.

"Amen." He opened his eyes and set his gaze on her.

For her part, she paid him little mind—setting her napkin to the side and scooping a large bite of eggs into her mouth. Only then did her eyes meet his.

"What?" Her words rubbed at him. "Is there something on my face?"

He shook his head. Quickly. No sense in keeping her agitated.

"Well then, I suggest you mind your food and your manners." Then she turned her attention back to her plate.

A bit stung, it took a few moments for him to pull his regard from her to his own meal. As he swallowed his first few bites, he puzzled on what he could do or say. Might he just come right out with it? Though the idea terrified him more than a little, he had nothing left.

"Darling," he started, setting his fork down.

She glared at him. "What?"

"I was just wondering if there was something wrong? You seem a bit...tense."

"Tense? Why I never..." Her stare belied her incredulity.

He put up his hands in a gesture of surrender. "I didn't mean that. I only wanted to ask if—"

She stood. The chair behind her wobbled a bit. Owen prepared for the clap of it landing on the floor, but somehow it remained upright. "I think I've had about all I can stomach."

What was that supposed to mean? Was she ill? Or did she refer to him?

He watched, helpless, as she stomped into the kitchen, tossed the rest of her meal in a bucket, and walked the now-empty dish to the dish bin.

She stood there, pressing her hand to her forehead.

He prayed once more for wisdom. Dare he approach her? Or would it be best to give her space? In the end, he was drawn to her side.

"I'm sorry," he said, as he set a hand to her shoulder.

She wiped at her eyes with the edge of her apron. "No, it's me. I should be apologizing. I'm not too pleasant this morning."

He wanted to naysay her but found he couldn't. That would be a lie. "Just tell me what's going on. Maybe I can help."

She turned to face him. "Not this time, you can't."

He searched her face for any indication, any hint about what might be bothering her so. And came up empty.

"It's time for me to get to the ranch." She shouldered past him and headed for the door. Would she not wish him farewell?

As he looked on, she grabbed for her coat and scarf but didn't seem to think twice about her apron still being on. Then she opened the door and stepped outside, letting the door close behind herself.

How would he discover the source of her trouble if she wouldn't tell him? Still, he was determined he would find out. And make it right. Whatever it took.

Owen had thought until his thinker seemed plum sore. What could have upset his sweet wife so? Not that she didn't have a streak in her. She did. Still, this wasn't like her.

He took a sip of his coffee—his third cup—and sighed. What was he to do if he couldn't figure this out? What would happen when she came home that evening? Could he manage another altercation like the one this morning?

A knock sounded through the small cabin.

Now, who could that be? He struggled to his feet—no small task after having sat for some time—and hobbled toward the front door. "Who's there?"

"It's Eugene."

Ah, his neighbor. He should have expected as much. The man dropped by regularly. Most every day in the last month. Perhaps, he was missing his son. Couldn't be easy to have healed that relationship just to have Dan go off to Tombstone to start his new life there.

"Coming," Owen called, though he wasn't moving as fast as he would like. "I'll be there in a minute."

The door handle jerked, and the barrier was removed. His dear friend stood in the opening, watching Owen struggle.

Eugene frowned. "Hip bothering you?"

As much as Owen wanted to deny it, there was no point. "Yeah. That and then some." He pivoted and moved back toward the table. "Come, sit a piece. I'll get you some coffee."

"No, sir. You sit, and I'll get it." His friend stepped into the great room and shut the door.

Owen glanced at Eugene's shaking hands. That tremor had been getting worse these last few months. And Owen worried after him. Perhaps, as much as Eugene worried after Owen. "Nah, I just need to work out a kink for a minute."

Eugene quirked a brow.

"Oh, come on. I'm not invalid. Not yet, anyway."

Eugene shrugged. "Let me know if you need an extra hand." The man sat at the table near Owen's cup.

It wasn't long before Owen returned to the table with a mug of fresh brewed coffee in hand. He set it in front of his friend and then lowered himself into his earlier vacated seat. Perhaps, he was more relieved than he let on to be off his feet. Still, from Eugene's expression, he would wager the man could guess.

"What's got you in a tizzy?" Eugene lifted the mug to his mouth.

Owen cringed as the hot liquid sloshed in response to the muscle twitches in the man's hand and arm. "I'm not in a tizzy."

The man took a sip and lowered his cup. "You most certainly are."

"What would I have to be upset about?"

"How should I know? That's what I asked you."

Owen frowned. After so many years of knowing each

other, the man read him all too well. He leaned forward on his elbows. "It's Dorothy. She's in a snit about something."

"Oh?"

"Yeah. She was short with me this morning, and…if I didn't know better…I'd think she was trying to pick a fight."

"Did she?"

"Did she what?"

"Manage to pick a fight?"

"No, sir. I'm no dummy."

Eugene smiled. "That's up for debate."

Owen gave the man an exasperated look. "What can I do?"

"Did you say something before she started acting strange?"

"I complimented her cooking is all."

"That can't be it." The man appeared thoughtful for a moment. "Maybe it's how you said it. Womenfolk get all concerned about how things sound."

Owen shook his head. "That's not it. I just know there's something else going on."

"She could just be having one of them days. Everybody does."

Owen nodded. Perhaps, that was the best they could come up with. And maybe, it was the truth. She was entitled to have a bad day every now and again. Still, something about it didn't set right with him. It gnawed at him.

"If you'd like, we could hitch up my wagon and surprise her at the Millers'."

Owen mulled on that for a moment. How would she react? Would she be upset he intruded? No, that wasn't likely. Perhaps, she'd be touched he made the effort.

Yes, that might work. He shifted his focus back to his friend. "Let's do it."

Eugene clapped his hands which, even when clasped, shook more than Owen liked. "It'll be good to see them youngins. They sure do grow fast."

Owen smiled. But something in the back of his mind remained unsettled about the whole thing.

Owen watched as his friend pulled at the reins and slowed the horse on their approach to the Miller homestead. Filled with trepidation as he was, it became difficult to think clearly. What would he find at the ranch? What kind of reception would he get from his wife?

He set the brake and maneuvered to lower himself from the wagon—always a bit of a struggle. But he'd much prefer the hardship to the embarrassment of having someone assist him.

Now with feet firmly on the ground, he made his best effort to catch his breath. And grumbled to himself about his infirmity. It was no use, though. Nothing would improve his situation. Nothing.

And while he couldn't help mutter his frustration, even that was futile.

He turned to find Amanda Miller standing at the top of the porch steps with little Oliver in her arms.

"Didn't expect to see you today." She smiled, but the lightness only barely touched her eyes. Did she know something? Were all the Miller women in a mood today?

He dismissed the idea. Truly, it was ludicrous. There were any number of reasons Amanda might be struggling today. It could be nothing more than fatigue, for all he knew.

"That's a fine-looking fella there" Eugene spoke up. He stepped closer to the base of the stairs.

Then Amanda's eyes reflected the brightness of a smile as she pressed a kiss to the small child's forehead. "Thank you. We like him."

"Where are the others? Off causing trouble?"

Her brow furrowed. "They're at school."

"Oh, yes." How had he been so thoughtless? Of course, the children would be minding their learning.

Owen shook his head and let out a small laugh. "Looks like we came a might too early, Eugene."

"Nonsense." The man looked over his shoulder as he climbed the few steps. "It's always a pleasure to sit with this fine lad."

Amanda's eyes fairly shone as she looked between Eugene and her son. Her demeanor had changed in those few moments. Owen believed she might even be glad they came.

But when her gaze landed on Owen again, there was something more concerning underneath. No mistaking it. Something was afoot.

The front door opened, and Dorothy's head appeared. "Who—?" Then recognition lit her face, and she turned to Amanda. "Were we expecting company?"

No 'hello, dear'? 'Good to see you'? Something truly was amiss.

"I believe this is some sort of pleasant surprise," Amanda said, stepping toward Dorothy. The slight stress on the word 'pleasant' did not escape Owen.

Dorothy frowned. "I've got my hands full today." She glanced at Owen. "Sorry, I can't stop right now." Then she disappeared from sight.

Amanda gave Owen a meaningful look. There would be a conversation forthcoming. And he didn't begrudge it. Any insight into what may be bothering his wife so would be much appreciated. The more he thought he understood women, the more he discovered he came up short.

"I'll get you two something to drink. Please, sit, enjoy the view." Amanda's smile filled her face, but again was vacant from her eyes.

Owen worked his way up the stairs and to a rocking chair on the porch, Eugene with him.

Amanda lingered for those few minutes. Was she uncertain he could manage on his own? She always did worry so.

Now that he was settled, she moved to the front door.

"You gonna let me hold that youngin'? We sure did come quite a ways for the chance."

Amanda turned back to him. After only a brief moment of thought, she walked the small one to her kin. "I'll be back in a minute."

He nodded. "I'm sure I can manage until then."

As she moved off after her errand, Eugene offered the young boy his finger. The little one eagerly reached for it and pulled the roughened digit toward his mouth.

"I wouldn't, if I were you," Owen warned. "Remember, his sister was a biter."

Eugene nodded and curled his finger, giving the child's hand a gentle tug. "He sure is sweet."

"Aren't they all?"

Eugene nodded.

"Wonder when that boy of yours will be a Pa." Owen loved the children at the ranch and wanted for even more. They were like his grandchildren, but they weren't truly.

The reminder that he would never have one of his own bothered. But the sting was not what it could be. Brandon did not treat Owen like anything but his children's grandpa.

Still, Eugene had hope. Dan and Lily had written that they had a young one on the way. One glance at his friend, and Owen knew he thought about the same thing.

Would the baby's arrival in a few months be reason enough for Eugene to pick up and move to Tombstone? Be closer to his family? Owen wouldn't be surprised. But he would miss his friend if the man did.

Amanda returned with two glasses in hand. Owen did his

best to balance the liquid-filled cup and the child, who reached for the new object.

It took only a few seconds to decide it wouldn't work. Not in this rocking chair. But Amanda reached for Oliver, relieving Owen of the bundle and his struggle.

She bounced the child on her hip and spoke soothing words to him—the very picture of what a mother should be. But as she glanced back toward Owen and Eugene, there was a hesitation about her. Was there something she wished to say? Was it difficult? Or perhaps, she didn't feel free to speak in front of Eugene?

Owen turned to his friend who, even then, was finishing his drink. That was fast.

"I'd like to take a gander at them horses over yonder." The man tilted his head toward the barn. Indeed, Owen could see at least one painted mare in the side paddock.

How could he encourage his friend without sounding like he wished for the man's absence? He couldn't. So, he just nodded while Eugene stood and moved farther down the porch.

Amanda watched him go as well.

"Please, my dear, sit. Take a load off. You look like you could use a minute."

A tight smile was her response. But she did take his advice and move around him to the recently vacated seat.

Silence filled the space between them. He didn't like it so well. But he tried to settle into it and give her the time she needed to share what was on her mind.

"I'm glad you came," she said at last.

He nodded.

"Cook has been...in a strange mood today."

He gazed out over the field. "That so?"

"Yes." Her regard leveled on him, but he didn't turn. No need to entertain one more woman's accusatory glare.

Amanda pushed out a breath. "She thinks you forgot her birthday."

Birthday? Owen wished the wooden planks beneath him would open up and swallow him. How could he have neglected something so important? And now, he had to admit that to Amanda.

"You did, didn't you?" Her words were soft.

There was no point in denying it. His reaction had clearly made his guilt rather obvious. So, he nodded.

She let out a sigh. But said nothing.

He thought for a moment. What could he do? He had to make up for his oversight, but also find an appropriate way to honor her day. And it seemed a bit late for that.

"I...am not sure how to fix this." After some more moments of silence, he turned to face Amanda.

A slow smile tugged at the corners of her mouth. "Asking for help is the first step."

He lifted his eyebrows. "Then I'm asking."

She set a hand on his. "And I'll do what I can to help."

Owen made his way to town. What would he find? What could he get that would compare to everything Dorothy did for him? He pulled the cart to a halt just outside the livery. But he set his sights on the General Store nearby. That would be the best place to find something. Wouldn't it?

In a matter of moments, he moved down the planked sidewalk and through the doors of the mercantile establishment. And minute after minute passed while he wandered the aisles. Passing by carvings and soaps and all manner of candy, he started to fret. It wasn't as if there would be a sign on anything that read 'Perfect Gift for Dorothy.' No, he'd have to do some thinking.

He sighed. The thinking he'd done today hadn't amounted to a hill of beans. Could he really be responsible for this task? Why hadn't Amanda given in and come herself? But no matter how he begged, this was what she decided—he would get the gift and the pie, she would prepare for their party.

Owen supposed he should be grateful the Lord Almighty graced their day with warmth and the absence of snow on the ground.

He shifted his focus back to the commodities around him. Why did women have to be so difficult to shop for? And why could he not have more time? It was his due, though. It had been his forgetfulness that got him in this fix.

As he turned the last aisle, he set eyes on the fabric table. He almost turned away, but something caught his attention— a beautiful blue with tiny flowers. Something about it struck him. Dorothy had always been drawn to blue. And it did seem mighty feminine with the buds peeking out here and there.

Maybe...just maybe...

All had been set. Owen had one more job to do. And he didn't relish it. Amanda had once again tasked him with the more difficult of the things needing to be done. While he wasn't a coward, facing down his wife in her mood wasn't something he was altogether prepared for. But he garnered what strength he did have and opened the door.

It wasn't enough.

As he stepped into the homestead, he caught the unmistakable sound of sniffling. And his heart fell.

Dorothy's mood had gone from sour to sad. That hurt him.

How would he approach her? Would she let him comfort her?

He made it a couple of steps before the creaking of the floorboards gave him away.

All sounds of her emotion halted.

He held his breath. Might she believe it nothing? Not likely.

Shuffling of feet neared, and she appeared in the doorway to the kitchen.

Their eyes met and held.

She turned away without a word. Was she so vexed?

He swallowed against a surprisingly dry throat. And pushed himself to move farther into the house. Once he reached the kitchen, he stopped.

Dorothy was peeling potatoes, her head down...no sense of acknowledging him. But she knew he had come into her space. The tightening of her shoulders told him as much.

He watched her for several moments more as she continued to ignore his presence. And he prayed—asking the Lord what he should do, begging for the gumption to see this through.

Filled with a new boldness, he stepped closer to his wife and set a hand on her back.

She pulled away.

"Dorothy..." He kept his voice soft.

"It's nothing," she countered. "Nothing at all."

"It's not 'nothing.' You're upset." Why would he not move forward with the plan and let things work themselves out? Did he feel the need to sort out something between them instead? Yes. Because his actions—or rather inaction—had hurt her.

"I don't want us to be like this," he said when he found his voice again.

"Like what?" She dropped the peeled potato and pressed her hand holding the knife to the pail.

"Pulling away from each other. Instead of holding on tight."

Her shoulders deflated, and her fingers touched her mouth. Did she fight tears once more?

"Tell me."

Her body shook.

"If you need to, let me have it. I can take it." His bravest words yet. He wasn't certain they were true.

"I just...feel overlooked." The last word was clipped as she worked to rein in her emotion.

Silence thickened the space between them.

"I know. And I'm sorry about that."

She continued to tremble.

"Look at me." He reached out and urged her to turn.

She resisted but dropped the knife and gave in. Her eyes betrayed her. There was a puffy redness underneath. "I know I shouldn't feel this way. But I don't know that anyone...cares to notice..." Her words were swallowed up by the hand pressing to her face.

"That's not true. *I* know. *I* see."

"Do you?" Her gaze held his, her feelings so raw...it took his breath for a moment.

The door behind him slammed against the frame.

"Cook, I need you!" It was Amanda. Had she given up on Owen's ability to summon Dorothy?

His wife wiped at her eyes and straightened her apron. Then she stepped around Owen. "Whatever is the matter, child?"

"It's Samuel. He's got a cut on his arm. I need some help calming him."

Dorothy's brows furrowed but only for a moment. Then

she seemed to set all else to the side as she moved toward the other woman. "Let's go. I'm behind you."

Amanda's eyes searched out Owen's. Their gazes locked, and she raised an eyebrow.

Was he ready to end their exchange, as tense as it was, to join a party? Would they lose all sense of what they had been discussing? For certain, Dorothy may never again admit her moment of weakness.

But he was helpless to stop either of the women as they moved onto the porch. He picked up step and hurried after them, doing his best to keep up as they moved across the yard toward the barn.

"Goodness, where is he?" Dorothy said as they moved faster.

"Just over here." Amanda paused and looked back at Owen.

"Y'all go on ahead," he called. "I'll be there in a minute." As much as he wanted to see Dorothy's face at the revelation of the party, he truly needed a moment to clear his head.

The two women disappeared into the barn, and Owen heard the shouts of "Surprise!" from that direction.

He allowed himself a slight smile. At least, his darling wife would know that she had not been neglected.

Bidding Eugene farewell as he maneuvered his cart away, Owen prayed his friend would make it safely to his cabin. Though Owen's attention was then drawn toward his own cart.

Dorothy sat on the bench, gushing her thanks and good-byes to Brandon and Amanda. "It was just the best birthday ever! Thank you."

Amanda shook her head. "Uncle Owen did most of the work. He wanted it to be special for you."

Dorothy's gaze met his. There was a softness there and a bit of sadness. Regret? How could he admit that this wasn't all what it seemed? Could he face her hurt again?

He pulled himself into the cart, pushing down the flaring pain in his hip. The last thing he wanted was for Brandon to feel the need to assist him. It took a bit longer than it should have, but Owen settled next to his wife soon enough.

"You'd best get home and rest," Amanda called. "And remember, don't come out here tomorrow. The day is for you to enjoy."

Dorothy nodded and looked away. She never did like to draw attention to herself. Owen could tell that, in that respect, the party had been a bit awkward for her. Still, no one could deny that she cherished the thoughtfulness of her friends.

"Get her home," Brandon directed to Owen. "And you two enjoy your day off."

Owen nodded as he picked up the reins. "Thanks for everything."

The Millers waved it off as if it were nothing. It meant so much to him—not just the party, either. But their care and consideration for him and Dorothy.

"See you on Thursday, then." Owen lifted the reins and set the horse into motion.

The ride back to their cabin was quiet. Maybe too quiet. But Owen was deep in thought. How to address this growing tension between him and Dorothy? Would it go away? Did he want it to? Or would it be best to face it?

They made it home in short order. He saw Dorothy down, and he stabled the horse before trudging into the cabin. His hip ached terribly, but he did not think he would get relief any time soon.

Stepping into the cabin, he listened for where Dorothy

might be. Nothing. But as he scanned the open area, he spotted her in her chair near the fire.

So, he might be able to get the weight off his leg sooner than expected. He settled into the chair beside her—his chair.

But it was still too quiet.

"Dorothy, I—"

"I need to say how sorry I am." Her words cut through his statement.

Her apologize? What for? But he knew.

"Here I was moping and being all selfish...and you had that wonderful party planned for me. And the beautiful fabric for curtains...I hate that I had such horrible thoughts about you."

Her words made him feel worse. He had to come clean.

"I mean, you must have—"

"Wait." He held up a hand. "It's not what you think."

Her brows furrowed as she continued to watch him. "Not what I think?"

"Well...there was a party, and I did plan it. With help. A lot of help."

"So...?"

"The truth is I did forget your birthday."

Her eyes widened, but she held her tongue.

He shifted in the seat until he faced her. "But it's not that I don't care, Dorothy. Can't you see? Every day with you is special. Every day is a gift."

Her mouth became a thin line.

"It's difficult for me, you see. 'Cause I want to treasure you each day that we have together."

Her expression didn't change except for a twitching of her lips.

He hung his head. "So, I'm sorry I let you down."

Her hand covered his. "That was...just beautiful."

His gaze sought hers.

Her features had softened, and a smile played at her mouth. Could it be that she understood? That she might forgive him?

"I do feel cherished. Every day."

He fought against a lump forming in this throat.

She leaned toward him and pressed a kiss to the side of his face. And then to his lips.

"You're the best thing that's ever happened to me, Dorothy."

"And you..." Her voice caught. "Were well worth waiting for."

Owen clasped her hands and together, they settled into a comfortable silence. All the while, his heart warmed at the knowledge that they would be okay. More than that—they had what it took to weather any storm.

And he was thankful. Enough for every day.

TRUST IS GOLDEN

Dorothy Miller fought the urge to snap the reins and encourage the aging horse to pick up her pace. But that would only increase the bumping of the cart. How would her own aging bones handle that?

As it was, they ached for home. For a comfortable seat and her sweet Owen to dote on her. Just thinking of him brought a smile to her face. It always did. The old coot.

The roof of their cabin peeked over the top of the hill. She was almost there.

Shaking and rickety, the wagon protested the final climb. But it was sturdy. Owen made certain of that. He wouldn't risk his Dorothy, as he said so often. Yes, he was a kind-hearted man...even if he was a lot of trouble.

She smiled to herself as she pulled up to the simple log structure that was their home. And then she waited for Owen to come out, greet her, and take the horse to the barn.

But nothing happened. No one came.

So, she waited.

And waited.

Was Owen all right? The old goat. He must be sleeping. Fine thing, that. She'd been working her hands 'til they calloused, and he was napping the afternoon away!

But she couldn't be cross with him. He'd had his share of hardship over the years. She couldn't begrudge him some peace and rest after what he'd put that body of his through in his younger years as a ranch hand. Too many years abusing it.

It took more effort than she'd have liked to stable the horse and secure the barn, but she did it. Without thinking bad thoughts about her husband. Well...not too many, at least.

She stifled a laugh in spite of the ache in her back. They did pick at each other. But that was their way.

Opening the door slowly, she glanced about the cabin. There were no lanterns lit within. As the sun began to set, the interior had dimmed.

She made quick work of remedying that. Then she tiptoed to the kitchen and pulled together a few foodstuffs to prepare a simple meal. Dare she rouse Owen to eat? Dare she not?

If there were one thing she couldn't abide, it was a stomach growling, complaining it hadn't been fed, on her watch.

Nope, she'd wake him all right. There'd be no tummy grumbles in her bed tonight.

She had just put the meager stew together and started it heating on the stovetop when a noise outside disrupted her concentration. Or what was left of it.

Who would visit at this hour?

"Owen!" she called. She would much rather he receive than her. It was best.

No response.

"Owen!"

Nothing.

Well now, didn't that beat all? He was dead asleep. She knew the kind. And it was just like him, too.

She wiped her hands on her apron and moved toward the door. But as she neared the window, she spotted a figure, blurred by the dimness and her declining night vision. The intruder moved into the barn.

The barn?

Was there a thief upon them? Come to steal their horses from right under their noses? The cad!

The man had another think coming if he thought she was going to stand by and let a common ruffian take her old mare. Why...she never!

"Owen!" she called again. Whatever was the matter with that man? Did he have cotton in his ears?

Uneasiness prickled at the skin on her arms, and she swallowed. Would it be up to her to defend their home? Could she do that?

She closed her eyes. *Dear Lord, give me the strength to do what I need to. And the sense to know what not to.*

Then she snatched her broom. A fine weapon. She'd beaten back many a beady-eyed mouse with it. But a horse thief was not a mouse.

Maybe they weren't so different, she told herself. Both bullies. Only this one was taller.

Movement beyond the window betrayed that the man came toward the cabin. Did he think this humble house had valuables? Would he try to harm her and Owen?

Even as she peered, she couldn't make out more than his form as he came closer. She pressed her back to the wall. No sense in giving away her position. She gripped the broom stick until her hands hurt. The moment that scalawag stepped in this house—*her* house—she'd whack him with this broom with all the force she could muster.

Yes, that was a good plan. Sound. Doable.

A thickness rose in her throat as the steps to the door creaked. She couldn't do this.

The door latch jangled.

She had to. She would. She raised the broom and closed her eyes. Wait...if she kept her eyes closed, how would she hit him square in his detestable face?

Open eyes. Yes, that was better.

The door swung inward and...

She brought the broom down. It smacked the door so hard it sent a tremor through her arms, and she landed solid against the wall, all the wind rushing out of her.

She gasped for breath.

Someone spoke to her.

In a gruff voice.

"Dorothy?"

Hands were on her arm.

She flung an elbow back.

There was a satisfying "*Hummpff.*"

She turned to face her attacker.

And there was Owen, working to catch his breath. *Owen?* How? Why? *How?*

"Oh dear!" She dropped the broom and grabbed for his arm to help him stay upright.

He held up a hand. "I'll be fine."

"I'm sorry...but you were a horse thief!"

He looked at her, an eyebrow quirked. "A horse thief? When? In a past life?"

"No...just now when I saw...well, you see, you...oh, never mind." Her cheeks burned, and she couldn't get the words out.

He rumbled.

Was he coughing? Fighting for breath? Had she killed him?

"Owen?" She grabbed for his arm.

He took her hand as he continued to shake, head down.

After some moments, he looked at her at last, his whole face lit up as he released his laughter.

Laughter? This was funny to him?

"Owen Miller, I might have killed you!" She shook off his arm.

He howled louder. "Most certainly, my dear. Seems I deserved it. And then some, I'm sure." His eyes gleamed.

"You most certainly did!" She crossed her arms. "You scared me something terrible."

His laughter faded, and he met her gaze. "I apologize. I had no idea you would be so concerned."

"Well, I thought you were asleep." She moved back to the kitchen to check on her stew. "I hadn't a thought who would be traipsing around in our barn at this hour. Unless it was someone up to no good." She shot him a look.

"Sounds like me, all right." He winked.

She picked up a wooden spoon and began stirring the stew. It had started to burn. Couldn't anything go right this evening? "I'm glad you're amused."

His smile faded, and he walked to her. "Don't be mad. I won't live long enough to work it off."

She couldn't help the grin that tugged at her lips when she peered at him. "Maybe. But you could try."

He rubbed her upper arms. "I hereby solemnly swear. I will work my hardest to make it up to you."

The grin that had threatened finally overcame her features.

"Til death do us part." His own smile filled his face.

She leaned into him and let the tension of the past several moments slip away. All was forgiven and forgotten. Except... where had he been?

Pulling back, she opened her mouth to ask.

"Shall I...set out the bowls?" He looked at the pot.

She found herself too tired and unwilling to further

muddy the waters with another discussion. Perhaps, it was his own business where he had been. Maybe he'd just been for a ride. Or over to visit Mr. Hayworth. It was no matter.

She sighed. "Hope you like your stew a little on the burnt side."

"I'll take it. As long as I get to sit at the table with you."

Several days later, Dorothy worked to clean the kitchen at the Miller house. At last, she put the remaining two dinner plates in the dish bin. A quick wash of the final implements and she'd be done.

"Now, you get on home," Amanda said, her voice bearing a gentle reprimand. "You have long since earned a decent rest."

"As if you haven't," Dorothy countered. Why was the woman forcing her out of the homestead's kitchen? Was she not welcome?

Dorothy chided herself. She knew better. That wasn't it in the least. Amanda Miller simply wanted to send her home early to enjoy the evening. That was all.

Then why didn't it sit well with Dorothy? Was it always so hard for her to be the receiver of such kindnesses?

Hands pressed against her shoulders, urging her toward the dining room.

"I meant what I said." Amanda's tone did not invite the retort already building within Dorothy. "Now, off with you."

Louise giggled from across the room.

Dorothy winked at the child as she grabbed for her shawl. "You are too kind to this old bird."

Amanda shot her a look that mocked a hard edge. "And you are too hard on yourself. You deserve an evening off every now and then. I can manage by myself just fine."

"But—"

Amanda held up a hand. "I won't hear it. Just go."

Though her words were edged, there was a smile on the younger woman's face.

Conceding defeat—not something she did easily—Dorothy nodded and, wrapping her shawl around herself, headed toward the front door.

At the last second, she turned. "Don't forget—"

"I won't!" Amanda yelled from the kitchen. A clanking sound told that she had begun scrubbing the plates. "For the love of all that's good and holy, Cook, just *go!*"

Without another word, Dorothy opened the door, slipped through, and headed out. It was only a matter of moments before she sat in the wagon, her sights set on her cabin. And only a half hour later, she paused at the front of the small structure to wait for Owen.

She waited.

And waited.

Where was he? This had become old news. More and more of late, he had not been home when she returned. He'd been consumed with errands. It was always something.

She slapped the reins and steered the animal closer to the barn. In short order, she was in her own kitchen stirring up something for their dinner. But when Owen might show up, she didn't know.

Surely, he would be home for supper. That had been a constant. Whether his business took him to visit a friend, or to the General Store, or wherever, he always made it home for the evening meal.

But now, she glanced across the cabin at the complete emptiness. The bare plates in front of the vacant chairs taunted her. Where was that man? Did he dare risk her ire by delaying his return?

And just where would he say he had been today? It was always different. Surely, he was running out of errands after all these days. There were not that many places to go in Wharton City.

The clomping of hooves outside drew her attention in that direction.

Ah ha! There he was...

At last.

She looked at her timepiece.

He came in just minutes before she would have been home on a normal day. Had he planned it to be so? And if that were the case, had he been out even on the days she arrived to find him home? Having just returned?

Something unpleasant stirred in her stomach. What was really going on with that man? Was he hiding something?

No, that didn't seem like him at all. He had always been an open book. Unless...

He had something he needed to keep from her.

Such as what?

She shook her head, unwilling to think on such things.

The door creaked, and he entered.

"Good evening to ya'." She stood in front of him, planted and ready for a confrontation.

His eyes connected with hers, grew wider, and the most sheepish smile tugged at the corner of his lips. "Why, Dorothy, I...um...didn't expect to see you home this early."

She nodded. "That's as plain as the broad side of a barn."

His eyebrows gathered. "W-what do you mean?"

She dropped her arms. "Aw, nothing. It's just curious is all."

"What's curious?" He broke their eye contact as he turned to close the door and secure the latch.

"I think you know what I'm talking about, Owen Miller." She wagged a finger at him before spinning toward the kitchen and moving in that direction.

Silence behind her told that he didn't follow.

"Your dinner's done got cold."

"Oh?"

"I ain't got no reason to lie." Her gaze on him was meaningful. Could she communicate her thoughts that way? Would he understand? Or was he too thick-headed? He wasn't always the best at noticing things like that. His mind just didn't seem to work that way. He was more...obvious. "Do you?"

He hobbled to the table. "Do I what?" His voice had become gruff.

Oh, well. So what, if he didn't like this conversation?

"Do you have any reason to be fibbin'?"

He paused as he lowered himself into his seat, his body caught between standing and sitting. "Why would you ask me a question like that?"

She shrugged and looked down at the beans. "No reason."

He stood once more. "You got a reason all right. Ain't no female ever asked a question she ain't got something she's aiming for."

Dorothy put a hand to her chest and inhaled sharply, feigning shock. As if he weren't right. He was, of course. But that didn't mean she had to let on that he was. "Why, Owen Miller, I'm surprised at you."

"At *me*?" he said, his voice rising. "I'm playing mouse to your cat here."

Dorothy clamped her mouth shut. She needed to think better before speaking again. No more of this childishness. She might as well ask him what she truly wanted to know. Sighing, she let out the building tension in her shoulders. "Where were you this afternoon?"

Something passed in his eyes. It also brought a twitch to his features. She would bet her life that he hid something. No way was he about to speak truth to her. Not a chance.

"I...was at the General Store."

"Yeah?" she challenged.

"Yeah."

She crossed her arms. "What'd you get?" Her eyes roamed over his person and around him. There didn't appear to be anything new.

"Ah..." He seemed to hunt for an answer. "Some pipe tobacco."

Her eyes narrowed. Shoot! He was quicker on his feet than she'd thought. But she'd do one better. "I thought that's what you got Monday."

"I, um, smoked it all."

She nodded. "You smoked it all, did you?"

He bobbed his head as he looked toward the floor.

"In two days?"

The silence in the room was thick.

"Well," she retorted. "One thing is certain. You have a bad habit forming."

He didn't look up.

"And it's one of two things."

He peered up at her, a brow quirked. Did he not catch her meaning?

"Smokin' too much. Or *lyin'*." With that, she stomped across the great room to their shared bedroom and shut the door soundly.

Dorothy spent much of the next day stewing. Not even her work at the ranch could distract her from her thoughts. What on earth was that man thinking? How could he lie to her? To *her*? It just wasn't right. They'd been married precious few years, and now he trampled on her trust? And Lord knew she didn't trust easily.

Lord knew...

If only Owen could understand that. She'd thought he did.

She squared her shoulders and shifted her focus to her task as the water started to boil.

It was clear—he didn't. Or wouldn't.

Movement near the door to the dining room gave her pause. She turned in that direction, but it was only Amanda with Oliver in her arms. The tune she hummed to soothe the little one was pleasant, but it did nothing to calm Dorothy's worn nerves. Still, she offered the younger woman a smile.

"Naptime?" Dorothy took a moment from her vegetables and stepped toward the mother and child.

Amanda nodded and sighed. "He's fighting it."

"Oh, not this one." Dorothy peered into the sweet angel face of the newest addition to the household. Then she glanced at Amanda, the weariness shown around her eyes. No matter how well her features could disguise it—Dorothy knew. "Still not getting a lot of sleep?"

Amanda drew in a deep breath. "Is it that obvious?"

Patting her friend on the shoulder, Dorothy gave her what she hoped was an encouraging smile. "Only to someone who knows you well. And cares deeply."

The younger woman nodded but didn't say anything. "I..."

"Yes?" Dorothy prodded when Amanda's next words were not forthcoming.

"I just..."

Dorothy squeezed her arm. "I know, dear." But she didn't. She'd never been in Amanda's place. But that couldn't stop her from trying her best to sympathize and support her friend.

Amanda's gaze caught Dorothy's. "And Brandon, he... tries. He really does."

Dorothy nodded.

"But...I don't know. It's just not the same."

"Ah, those Miller men." Dorothy let her own emotions simmering underneath the surface show for a minute. "They have a stubborn streak, indeed."

Amanda nodded and looked back at the child, whose lower lip poked out and brow creased. He would be squalling soon. She bounced the bundle gently. The youngster did not relent.

"Even Oliver here, it comes natural."

Her words were not helping. That was obvious. Was she too stuck in her own troubles with Owen? This wasn't about her and Owen. This was about Amanda and what was happening with her.

Dorothy put a hand on the child's light curls. "They mean well, though—our Miller men. Can't fault 'em one bit for their good intentions. They got buckets of that."

Amanda did not take her eyes off Oliver or slow her rocking motions, but her demeanor seemed to lift. Dorothy's words couldn't change that the little one needed Amanda throughout the night, but perhaps they helped her perspective on some of Brandon's behavior...whatever was happening there.

"Oh, I think he's settling," Amanda whispered.

Dorothy looked down. "So, he is."

"Thank you." The words were mouthed as Amanda turned toward the hall.

Dorothy watched her go, hoping the woman would grab some sleep for herself. Yes, those men of theirs were tiresome and frustrating, but their hearts were always in the right place. And that included Owen.

She frowned. Did that mean she would have to be patient and understanding? Maybe give him space to show her that *his* intentions were good?

Blast it all!

Dorothy directed the horse's movements home. Not that her efforts were necessary. The horse knew the way. Most certainly. But it gave her a sense of purpose. Even when Owen was at the reins. He needed direction, too. That man would have them halfway to California if she wasn't watching him closely.

But as she neared the cabin, she was determined to be understanding. Determined to be patient. No matter what. Whether he was home. Or not.

After all, if he wasn't at the cabin, there must be a good reason. She had to trust him. And she did.

Didn't she?

This just wouldn't do. She *did*, for goodness sakes. It was up to her to quiet this crazy backtalk her mind was giving her. Or was it her heart?

As she pulled the cart to the log structure, she didn't wait for Owen to come out for the horse and wagon. She maneuvered the animal toward the barn, put the mare in her stall, and secured the cart for the night.

Then she headed into the cabin. She entered to lanterns set dimly. Still, it was light. Was Owen home?

"Owen?" she called.

"Yes?" he answered from the back sectioned-off area that made for their bedroom.

"You all right?" Her concern teetered on worry, but she managed to keep it in check.

"Yeah. Just getting this old body a-movin'."

She let out a breath. At least, he was home and whole. They'd managed his troubles with his hip rather well. And she refused to think what it might be like if it got worse.

As she moved toward the stove, the floors creaked. She needed to warm something for dinner. Maybe they could have something cold. It had been a long day. The need for coffee was great, but the desire for a good night of sleep overruled it.

No sooner had she put a pot on the stove then the hunkering steps halted behind her.

"Well, hello."

She turned. "Hello?"

With nothing further, she went back to pulling the few things together for a sauce.

"That's it?" Owen's voice was more gruff than usual.

"It?" She didn't look up from her work. Was she tired? Or just keeping her emotions in check? Besides, what could he mean? Was he cross about something?

"Let's see...last I saw of you, you accused me of smokin' too much or lyin'. Then, if memory serves, you stomped off and slammed the door."

Dorothy stopped her vegetable chopping. "Oh, that."

"Yeah. That. Is there something we need to talk about?"

She met his gaze. There was not anger there, but confusion and concern. She didn't have time for that.

Her focus returned to the cutting board. "No. I was just... in a mood."

"Mood?"

She kept cutting.

"Well..." His voice trailed off. Then nothing.

Heat crawled through her. Would he just stand there and stare at her? What was in his head?

She shot a glare at him. "Owen Miller, I declare! If you have something to say, I'd rather have you get it out."

Even as she continued to stare him down, she flinched. This wasn't at all how she thought this evening would go... how she *wanted* this evening to go. What was she doing? She had determined to be gracious and peacemaking. No matter what the old goat did to earn her ire.

"I..." he started.

She folded her arms across her chest. Why was she putting up such a front?

Owen held up his head. "I just wanted to ask you to the Valentine Dance on Saturday."

What had he said? The Valentine Dance? Was he asking her to the Valentine Dance? Right *now*? He really was a mystery.

He stood his ground, eyebrows raised.

Was he truly waiting for an answer?

She had never wanted to full out sass a man in her life so much. Really give him a piece of her mind.

But something in her held back. Something that was softened by her conversation with Amanda. The part of her that knew Owen better. That *knew* his heart was always in the right place when it came to her.

"I...would like that." She managed to get out.

"Now, don't go doing me any favors."

"You know better than to think such a thing." She almost cracked a smile. "Go on and set out a couple plates. If you want to eat tonight, that is."

He was a mess. *Her* mess. Somehow, she'd have to figure out what to do with him.

It had come—the Valentine Dance. Dorothy didn't know what to expect. Owen had been especially distant the rest of the week. Hardly home...and when he was, he had been tired and overall non-responsive. Once again, she found herself wondering what might be going on with the man.

But it was no matter. Every couple married more than two years or so had their better times and their worse. That was the whole reason for that part of the vows, right? Must be.

Dorothy situated her mama's cameo pin at the base of her

neck and played with the buttons of her bodice once more. But there was nothing more to be done with her appearance. It was what it was, take it or leave it.

Shaking her head, she forced a smile as she looked in the hand mirror. What did Owen see when he looked at her? What did she want him to see?

She put the reflective piece down. Best leave well enough alone.

Grabbing for her shawl, she took a breath and opened the bedroom door. She stepped into the great room to find Owen sitting in his chair. Just waiting for her as he always did, that contemplative look upon his face—so deep in thought his eyes were closed. Was he thinking of the things that had passed between them these last days? Or thinking on…

A great snore erupted from him.

She scowled. How rude! Had he no concern after these things at all? Stepping to his chair, she reached down and pinched his arm.

He startled awake. "Wha—?"

She put on her most innocent front. "Did I wake you?"

"Naw." He rubbed his eyes. "I wasn't sleeping."

She rolled her eyes but caught a glimpse of him smoothing over the spot near his shoulder where she got him.

He looked at his upper arm as if he could see it. Thankfully, it was well out of visual range.

"Shall we go?" she pressed.

"Oh." He looked up from his musings, stood, and opened an arm wide for her to pass. "Yes. I've got your chariot ready."

She nodded and walked in front of him, working to keep her feelings in check. No need getting all emotional. She would just have to see what this evening brought.

Moments later, they were perched on the wagon's bench and Owen spurred the old mare into action. They traveled in silence, with the exception of the times she needed to help

Owen stay on track. What would become of that man if she weren't there to assist him? How did he ever manage to get from the Miller Ranch to Wharton City and back without her?

They arrived at last to the small town that was still very much alive with merrymaking for this special occasion. After securing the horse and cart, Owen escorted her to the café where the festivities were in full swing.

They spent the first several minutes greeting those they knew, catching up on who had done what over the last couple of weeks, who fared well, and who needed to be looked in on. Such was the stuff of this small-town life.

Dorothy found herself deep in conversation with the mercantile owner's wife, her eyes straying often to the twirling of lace and fabric nearby as ladies moved about on the arms of their partners. How she wished Amanda could have made it tonight. But she knew that if the woman could have respite for an evening, she would likely use it for sleep. There was little doubt in Dorothy's mind, however, that Brandon had planned a Valentine evening plenty special for her.

Yes, those Miller men were crafty...and sweet at their core. Even if they needed minding.

As her thoughts turned in that direction, she shifted her focus toward Owen. But, as she spun, she could not catch sight of him anywhere.

"Excuse me," she said to the woman, who had continued to chatter on. "I don't want to be rude, but I seem to have lost my husband."

"Mr. Miller?" the woman asked, her features contorting.

"Yes. He was just here. I'm sure of it."

"Why, yes, he was. He probably just went to take his place for the next song." The woman's concern seemed to fall not on Owen's disappearance but on Dorothy's confusion. Why was that?

"Pardon? His place?"

"Yes. He has a part in this next song."

"A part?" Dorothy was more befuddled than ever. What was this woman saying? Surely, she was mistaken. Owen had not a musical bone in his body. What could he possibly—?

"Ladies and gentlemen," the mayor announced.

Everything stilled, and everyone turned their attention to where the man stood in front of the small band.

"Thank you all for coming out to celebrate with your sweethearts."

There were excited murmurs throughout the crowd.

Dorothy had a difficult time following along. She continued to scan for Owen, her worry spiking. That man had another think coming if she got ahold of him. Wander away and scare her like this! Had he gone soft in the head?

"We have the specific honor this evening to share a gift one of the well-established citizens of our town wishes to bestow on his sweetheart."

Dorothy vaguely heard the words but couldn't process much of what was happening. A cold sweat trickled on her skin. Was he well? Was he somewhere...hurt and unable to call for help? Was it his hip?

"...turn it over to Mr. Owen Miller."

What? She jerked her head around so fast she felt a twinge in her neck. But there he was—Owen—stepping into the mayor's place. What was he about?

His eyes were on her.

"I wanted to give my Dorothy something this Valentine's Day that went beyond some knick knack or trinket that, let's just say it, neither of us need. So, I thought on it. And, at my age, the ideas don't come as often as you'd think."

Laughter filtered around her. But she didn't laugh. She couldn't decide what she felt—so many emotions coursed through her. And so fast, she wasn't sure she could lay claim to one.

"So, I decided to surprise my Dorothy, my bride. Her father was a banjo player. And she loved that about him. In her family, gathering around and singing and dancing to his banjo playin' was what they did. I think it spoke love to her."

Dorothy froze. And she remembered those evenings of listening to her father's stories and how his music filled their tiny home. She always felt safe, cared for, and a part of something during those times. Her chest tightened.

"And I knew then...I had to learn to speak love to her." He picked up a banjo.

What was he doing? He didn't play. Had never played.

He lifted it into position as the band behind him raised their instruments. True, he seemed a bit awkward at first. But the world fell away when he began to play a favorite tune from her childhood. And then his deep baritone filled the space with the melody.

He was singing...to her.

What was holding her upright? Her heart clenched and beat harder at the same time. And warmth filled her whole being.

"That's a mighty fine man there." The mercantile owner's wife was at her side still.

Dorothy mumbled something. Seemed incoherent. Her focus was on Owen.

"How he learned that in just a couple of weeks, I'll never know."

She turned to look at the woman. "What?"

"Yes. He's been coming into town, sitting with my husband for two weeks. About every day, I reckon. Trying to get this song just right."

Dorothy's gaze fell on Owen again as he let the last notes of the tune fade.

His eyes found hers in the midst of the crowd, and he gave a slight bow.

The audience cheered.

Owen nodded and backed behind the band.

"Thank you, Mr. Miller," the mayor said, stepping forward. "That was some fine pickin', don't you think, folks?"

But the words dulled in Dorothy's ears. She maneuvered past the woman at her side without excusing herself. And then seemed to float around and through the remaining gathering until she faced her husband.

Once she was toe-to-toe with him, she lost her words.

"Did you like it?" he asked. His eyes gleamed like a schoolboy's.

She opened her mouth but couldn't speak. So she nodded, reaching for his hand.

"You all right?" His brow furrowed.

She nodded, looking down before meeting his gaze again. "I never expected...that is, no one has ever done something like that for me."

He pressed his free hand to the side of her face. "I ain't 'no one,' Dorothy. I'm your husband."

"So, you are." She smiled and choked back a sob. "And I've been so wrong. I thought...well, it doesn't matter what I thought. I was wrong. I should have trusted you. I do trust you. I just let my mind play tricks on me, and I—"

"Wait. Say that again."

"I trust you," she said, squeezing his hand. "And I do. I won't doubt again."

He stepped closer, a grin widening his features. "No, I mean the part before that."

She narrowed her eyes. "You mean the part when I said, 'I was wrong'?"

"That's it."

The urge to slip back a step and let him have it filled her.

But the playful glint in his eye melted her. "You get to have it this time, Mr. Miller. I *was* wrong."

He kissed the tip of her nose. "And it don't matter. If possible, I love you more."

This man...he made no sense. He must be crazy. But she embraced him and thanked the Lord that they had years ahead to be crazy together.

March

THE GOLDEN RULE

Dorothy rose early to welcome the sunrise. Her custom on this day each year. As light crept over the horizon, she hummed a tune. Not just any tune—a song of praise. For today was perhaps the most important day memorialized in all of creation. This was Easter Sunday.

Her eyes homed in on the farthest hill as the sun burst forth and the sky exploded with light. The darkness was banished in a beautiful splendor of color. As had been the darkness in her at one time.

"Just marvelous." The voice came from behind her.

She turned to find her husband staring beyond her toward the same miracle. He had joined her? How long had he been standing there? Had she disrupted his sleep when she eased out of bed this morning?

His eyes settled on hers, and he stepped closer. "Happy Easter."

A smile played at her lips. "Happy Easter." She wanted to chastise him for feeling the need to wake so early, but it wasn't in her. In truth, she was glad he decided to witness the coming day with her.

"I thought we agreed last year that you would wake me." His eyes shone, more with humor than anything else, but she discerned the gentle chastisement in his words.

"I..." she started but found her throat dry. "You seemed so peaceful. I didn't want to take you from your rest."

He gathered her into a loose embrace. "But *this* is where I want to be. With you."

She nodded, conceding that they had planned such. And her chest expanded to know that he saw her—her desire to honor this day above any other from sun up to sun down. Goodness, she loved this man.

As he pulled back only far enough to look down at her, she noted his attire. "How on earth did you dress so quickly?"

His brows waggled. "I have many talents, Mrs. Miller. Some you have yet to see."

"Oh?" Now her grin widened.

"I like to think of it as keeping a little mystery in our marriage."

She chuckled. He always knew just what to say to elicit a laugh. One glance at him and she noted, as usual, that he rather enjoyed her levity.

Owen turned his attention back to the far hillside and let out a deep sigh. "What a day, what a day."

She nodded and rested against him, his arm around her. God's blessings overflowed for certain. As the moment grew into several, her desire to remain intensified. But her awareness of the time caught up to her, and she leaned away from him.

He resisted releasing his hold but did so. "You got somewhere to be?" His lips tilted in a smirk.

"As it turns out, I do."

He frowned.

"I got so much to do before breakfast it would turn your head till it came plum off your body."

"Anything I can do?"

She gave him a hard look.

He lifted surrendering hands. "I know, I know, I'm not to be in your kitchen."

Part of her stuttered within at the comment. Was she so possessive of her domain? But she knew it was a fact. And one she wasn't apt to put to the side. *Know thyself, indeed.*

She put a hand to his chest. "You could get yourself cleaned up for church. Do your best to tame that hair. And then ready the wagon."

His whole being lightened. "Now that, I can do." He leaned forward and pressed a kiss to the side of her face.

The temptation to relax into him once more and linger in the moment was nearly overwhelming. But she resisted. Her mental list of tasks stilled her movements.

Owen shifted toward the cabin and, keeping one hand to the small of her back, he lifted the other in the direction of the front door. Once again, he knew her need to get on with the list and supported her in just the way she needed.

They climbed the couple of steps into their home and she made for the kitchen, pulling out a skillet for breakfast preparations and then checking on the rising bread dough. Today would be perfect. She would make sure of it. She grabbed for a few eggs and stepped back to the stove. Her husband would be ready for his morning meal in no time. So, she set some strips of bacon in the skillet and got started

"That's a pretty tune."

Where had that come from? She jerked her head toward the sound. Owen stood just where she had left him by the front door. And he watched her. Whatever for?

"Owen Miller, you're supposed to be cleaning up."

He crossed his arms. "Well, stop singing like that. How's a well-meaning fella supposed to ignore such a sound?"

Singing? Had she been singing? She eyed him.

He let his arms fall. "Aw…I didn't really mean for you to stop."

"You do beat all. Now, get before I change my mind about making your breakfast."

He held his hands up as if in surrender once more. Then his controlled expression opened until he was beaming.

"I mean it—get." She shooed him with her free hand.

He ducked into the bedroom.

She shook her head. He sure did beat all. Turning her attention once more to the bacon, she pressed it, savoring the sizzling response and the aroma that wafted through the entire cabin. It was nearly done. She'd best put the eggs on.

As she set the bacon to the side, she caught a hint of movement against the far wall of the kitchen. When she turned her focus toward it, light shimmered off the long, scaly body. And she screamed.

Uneven footsteps pounded on the floor.

She was frozen in place. The curled-up animal that had invaded her territory just stared. So, she kept screaming.

"Dorothy!"

The sound of her name was barely audible above the thudding of her heartbeat in her ears.

"Dorothy, are you hurt?"

Something touched her shoulder, and she jerked away, barely holding onto consciousness in her fright. But a hand grabbed her arm and held her fast.

She looked in that direction. It was Owen. The lines of his face had deepened, reflecting his concern. Shaking her head, she bit at her lip to stifle her cries. And pointed a trembling hand at the offending creature.

Owen was standing between her and the snake in the next

second, but he faced her and held to her arms. "It's all right. It's not going to hurt you."

She fought to keep control of her emotions. And only somewhat succeeded. "It's in my kitchen."

He grimaced. Surely, he knew that if he wasn't permitted in her kitchen, the creepy animal wasn't allowed either.

"I want it out. Now. Gone. Dead."

"Dead?" His voice betrayed a reluctance she didn't understand.

"It attacked me. Clear as day."

"Oh, I doubt that. It's just trying to find some warmth."

She frowned. This was war. "I cannot abide it, Owen."

"How about I take it outside and let it go, so it can—"

"Then all its snaky friends will think they can just…" She shuddered. "…slither in here and invade my kitchen."

Her gaze did not move from her husband. Was there evidence in his features that he thought her ridiculous? He chewed at his lip. Because he was thinking or because he held back a laugh?

Heat filled her. "I don't expect you to understand. But I want that thing gone. For good."

For a moment, she wondered if Owen would answer her. And if he did, would he give in? At length, he shrugged his shoulders and stepped toward the snake.

She threw her hands over her face. "I can't watch."

His footfalls paused. He must think her strange. But she didn't care. Any time she even thought about the animals, an eerie feeling came over her, and she could practically feel the things crawling on her.

Shivering, she made a small opening with her fingers and peeked out. Owen's back was to her as he hunched over.

Tightening her fingers against each other, she shut out the world again. Would there be some awful…thrashing? Or a yelp from Owen when the thing bit him? But the sound of Owen's uneven step—unhurried—was the only thing that she could discern.

Had he left her alone with the creature? Abandoned his silly wife? It took all the courage she could muster to lower one hand and peer over her fingertips.

And nothing.

The vile thing was gone. Had it truly done so with no resistance? Or was her husband some kind of snake charmer?

She stared at the spot near the corner where the icky animal had been. And there she remained until Owen returned.

He stepped over the threshold. "It's done."

She swallowed. Hard. Then croaked out her gratitude. "Thank you."

His brown eyes were soft on hers, lingering before he shifted his focus and moved back toward the bedroom.

The meal preparations called, but she needed a moment to calm her skittering pulse. If she could.

It had been an hour or better since the awful incident. The morning had continued, and they had made their way to church. But, even through the singing, even as the preacher took his place, Dorothy could not stop returning to the unpleasantness in her mind. And the unease filled her anew.

As if sensing it, Owen reached for her hand, clasping it, warming it.

She gave him a glance and even managed a small smile.

His eyes were gentle and understanding. Of course, they were. He loved her. All of her...even with her extreme aversion to creepy things.

He squeezed her hand once more, then released her to turn his Bible to First John as instructed.

She did her best to tune her thoughts to the reverend's words. Being Easter Sunday, she was not surprised he spoke of Jesus and His purpose on earth. Then Reverend Mason eased his weight back from the pulpit and straightened his jacket. That's what he always did before he brought his sermon to its point. She prepared herself for the man's rising tenor to reach a volume that enabled him to drive his message home. However, when he continued, he maintained the same gentleness he had been using.

"I am certain that there's not a person here that doesn't understand trials and suffering."

Dorothy's mind returned to her morning. A trial? Hardly. But it had left an impression on her that was not easy to shake.

"Some have experienced more than others. And the thing I find over and over is the tendency for trials to produce fear. Fear of future recurrence. Fear of the unknown. Fear of life."

Had he read her mind? Fear. It was real for her. Real to her. Where was he going with this? She prayed he wouldn't be dismissive. Perhaps, he might even offer some hope for her chronic fear of the beady-eyed things.

"But Christ came to set you free. From sin, most certainly, but free in other areas of your life as well. The passage tells us that 'perfect love casteth out fear.' Because of Christ, we have access to this perfect love. Let Him overshadow you with the peace that can only be found in that love."

Dorothy had heard this verse a million times, but it had never penetrated her heart like it did in that moment. Could she let God have her fear? Let Him give her peace, despite the presence of the slimy animals?

And what would that mean? Though the serpent was not glorified in Scripture, it was one of God's creations. He had formed it and set it on earth for a purpose. Perhaps, she should find some respect in her heart for that fact alone and let them be. She shivered at the thought of what turning a blind eye on the snake in her kitchen might have wrought. Maybe it would have been best, however, to let Owen put it outside. Instead of levying a death sentence upon it.

Heaviness filled her heart. What had she done? What had she required of Owen?

And how could she make it right?

Dorothy waved to Amanda Miller as Owen jerked the reins and the horse sped up. She watched behind her until there was no longer any hint of the church on the horizon. Only then did she turn and look at her lap.

How was she to go about this? Surely, if she opened her mouth, all of her guilt would spill out. And she would make herself even more ridiculous.

"You're quiet." Owen's comment lingered in the air between them.

Was he trying to say something more? Did her lack of conversation affect him so? Or was it that she usually chattered on so much that her silence now was noticeable?

She met his gaze. And shrugged.

He arched his brows. "Something on your mind?"

"Just thinking about what the preacher said." Even she knew her voice quivered.

His brows came together, and he slowed the horse until it stopped. "What's wrong?"

The emotion rising in her, thick in her throat, cut off her ability to speak. So, she shook her head.

He set a hand to her arm. "What is it?"

She reached for her handkerchief—which had been at hand almost since the preacher had started. Trying to speak, the noise sounded closer to a chirp than anything.

"You're getting me all worried." Owen pulled her closer

with an arm around her shoulders. "Whatever is the matter, we can make it right."

Except they couldn't. The deed had been done. Would anything make it right?

"It's...nothing...important," she managed.

"It sure is important!" His words were at her ear. "If it has you this upset, it's important to me."

She played with the fabric of the handkerchief in her lap. Perhaps, if she refused to look up, he wouldn't see how much she was bothered.

When she couldn't stand it any longer, she peered in his direction. From his expression, she could tell that he knew.

Her eyes brimmed with moisture. She waved a hand in front of her face as if that would ward them off. "It's just something Reverend Mason said."

"What?" His words were rather exasperated. "What is it?"

She bit at her lip. But it didn't matter. The truth burst out of her. "I did something awful. *We* did something awful." As she turned, she could hardly make out his concern through the blurriness.

"Dorothy," he said, his voice now taking on a harder edge, "It can't be this bad. Just tell me."

Then it occurred to her—something that might ease her guilt. Maybe even help her release it to God, knowing she had done all she could.

She sniffled, wiping at her eyes and clearing her vision. "We have to bury the snake."

"What?" Owen fairly spat out. "We have to what?"

"It's the only way."

"Help me out here. I'm a little lost."

"I let my fear take hold of me and then you—we—killed one of God's creatures. For no good reason. Just because I was afraid."

His eyes softened. "Oh, my dearest Dorothy," he said, pulling her even closer.

Though she desired his comfort, she didn't deserve it. So, she pushed back a little. "We just have to, Owen. We can't undo it. But this might make it right."

"Don't get all upset again. God knows about your fear. He understands."

She stared at her husband. "That doesn't make what we did okay by Him."

He nodded. "I know. But we can change our choices from here on. Look to Him for comfort when you're fearful the next time."

"And we can give that poor creature a proper burial."

Owen gave her a strange look. Did he think her strange?

"Don't look at me like that. I have to do what I can to let God know I've repented."

Her husband let out a long sigh. "Dorothy, we can't do that."

"Whyever not?" Her voice took on a higher pitch, and a fire lit in her belly. She may sound a little crazy, but she hadn't expected Owen to outright refuse to help her. Setting her chin and straightening her shoulders, she looked forward. "If you won't help me, I...I'll do it myself."

There was a hint of a chuckle in his voice when he said, "Look at me."

She crossed her arms and maintained her forward stare.

"Look at me." Now, his voice was more serious.

Though she wanted to resist in defiance, she knew he loved her. And wanted what was best for her. She had to give him the benefit of the doubt. That didn't mean she had to like it.

Turning to face him, she fought against the lump in her throat and the twisting of her mouth. She would not cry again.

Owen's gaze was soft and kind. "Neither of us can bury that snake. No matter how much you want to. No matter how much I want to do it for you."

She bit the inside of her lip, determined to hold back the sass that wanted to break forth.

"Because I didn't kill it."

Her eyes seemed to widen of their own accord. "What? You didn't—"

He grabbed for her hand. "I couldn't. The snake was harmless. And I didn't have it in me to hurt it."

That familiar fear crept into her once more. But she pushed it back, reminding herself about God's love. And reciting the Golden Rule to herself. It may not perfectly apply here, but she would want the snake to let her go about her life. That was how she wanted to respond to it.

She collapsed against her husband. "That's the best thing I've heard today!"

Owen's chest rumbled with laughter.

Then she pulled back. "You are just the sweetest man alive."

A smile spread across his face. "Just don't let that get around. It'll ruin my reputation as an ornery old man."

She swatted at his shoulder. "Owen Miller, you sure do beat all."

"Shall we forget this nonsense and go home? I've a hankering for some of those biscuits."

Moving away just a bit, she put a hand to his arm. "But if I ever see another one of those creatures in my house..." Her voice held a warning.

"You don't have to tell me twice."

Then she locked her arm through his and let her husband's warmth and God's peace fill her.

April

THE GOLDEN STANDARD

Owen Miller stepped into the cabin he shared with his wife. The aroma of their dinner filled his senses. It was delightful. How had he lasted so many years without this kind of greeting? Oh, yes, he hadn't. For so many years he had kept his admiration of the Miller Ranch's cook a secret. But the delicious smells of her talent in the kitchen had been his to enjoy.

Why had he waited so long to let her know how he felt? It seemed silly now. But at the time there had been reasons. Only, he couldn't remember them anymore.

His gaze landed on his Dorothy as she moved about the kitchen area, her back to him. He stepped in that direction, deciding he was well within his rights to interrupt her for a brief kiss. Anything longer, and he'd be in danger. She did not abide being disrupted well at all.

He managed to slip in behind her. How, he wasn't sure. His footsteps were far from silent. Still, he was thankful for the chance to be near her. Slipping his arms around her waist, he pressed a kiss to the side of her face.

And she sniffled.

Sniffled?

He attempted to look into her face, but she turned toward the stovetop, stirring a pot of some sort of green vegetables. Perhaps, she only suffered from hay fever. Spring was indeed in the air.

She wiggled out of his grasp and continued to shift here and there.

He decided to take himself to the dining table. Any help he offered would be declined. And not appreciated.

But as he sat, he thought he heard more sniffling. Turning his attention back to her, he watched as she rubbed at her face. Was she...crying?

What could he do about that? He did not care much for woman tears. They pulled at his heart and made him feel altogether helpless. He had learned well enough that her feelings were closer to the surface than he'd thought. And he could not just ignore her. That was unthinkable. He prayed for direction. How was he to approach her?

As he lifted his petition for wisdom, it occurred to him that he could just broach the subject. She might not respond well, but it was a start.

"You all right?" he blurted out. It wasn't the best attempt he had ever made. He grimaced.

There was a pause. Her shoulders rose and deflated with a long sigh. "Yeah." Then she went back to her work.

Dare he naysay her? It was evident that something wasn't right. Could he let it alone? He might should, but his heart ached. No way could he rest until he was satisfied that this was indeed nothing.

"You don't seem all right." His next attempt was not much better than his first. Had he not gained better experience with these matters?

She stopped. "I am fine, I tell you." But her voice wavered with emotion.

He struggled to his feet, part of him wishing to stay just as he was. Stepping toward her, he measured his movements as if she were a skittish doe. When he was but a pace or two behind her, he reached for her shoulder. "Look at me."

She shook her head.

"Come on, darling, look at me." He tugged her arm to encourage her to turn.

After a brief moment, she relented. Only...when she spun toward him, her hands flew to her face, covering her eyes. How was he supposed to discern anything like that?

"Dorothy?"

Her shoulders shook. Causing his concern to heighten. He opened his mouth, but she cut him off.

"It's just awful...the worst thing ever." Her words came out all of a sudden as she lowered her hands.

Then he saw the red-rimmed eyes she had been trying to hide. His chest tightened. What had happened? Had someone died?

"Tell me," he insisted.

She bit at her lip. Why was she so reluctant?

When she released her lower lip, the words tumbled out. "The ranch hands hated my compote."

Two thoughts flew through his mind: one, had the ranch hands known they hurt her feelings? And two, what was a compote? Stuck between these things, his next words didn't come before hers did.

"I...I try and I try, but I can't seem to measure up."

Now, that was nonsense. Those boys cared about her. As did the Millers. No one could argue that they appreciated her. "That's not true."

She sniffled again but avoided looking into his eyes. "I suppose you're right."

There now, that was better. Wasn't it?

"I guess I'm just...not..." Tears ran down her face again.

His chest squeezed. "Not what?"

"Not as good a cook as Amanda."

What? Not as good as Amanda? Why the need to compare herself to Brandon's wife? They were such different people. Besides, there was no way Dorothy's cooking was in question.

"Now, slow down." He rubbed her arm and led her toward the dining table. "Tell me what happened."

She resisted his prompting at first, but soon let him usher her to sit. "I worked all morning on a fruit compote for the boys, and when I brought it out, they wouldn't even touch it."

Finally, her gaze lifted to Owen's. And he saw just how upset she was. Something else was going on here. It wasn't like his Dorothy to be so easily bothered.

"Are you sure they knew what it was?"

"I..." She pursed her lips. "I don't know."

"To be fair, *I* have no idea what on earth you are talking about."

She gave him a stern look. "It's like jam."

"Them fellas are not fancy. Maybe you should've just called it jam."

She crossed her arms. "They don't turn their nose up at Amanda's cooking. Ever."

"Has she ever tried to serve them compote?"

Her glare shot daggers at him.

He held up his hands in surrender. "Forget I asked that."

After a moment, she dropped her gaze. "I suppose I'm just not—"

"Now, you stop that. Those boys love your cooking. *And* they like Amanda's cooking. Why do you need to be better than or not as good as someone else? Just be my darling Dorothy."

She gave him a sideways look. It seemed as if she didn't— or wouldn't—believe him. And he had run out of arguments.

Sighing, she slapped her hands to her legs. "You're right."

He tried to hide his surprise at her statement.

"I can be happy to just be ole' me."

"There you go." He realized how that sounded. "Being you is plenty good enough."

She stood. Had she heard his last statement? It didn't seem so. But she pressed a kiss to his forehead. "I need to get your vittles ready. I'm sure you're mighty hungry."

He couldn't argue with that, but he wanted to. Couldn't he make her feel any better than this?

She turned back toward the kitchen and moved off in that direction.

Did she feel better? He couldn't tell. Something in him deflated. Perhaps, he hadn't given her what she needed. But he was at a loss as to what more he could do.

Looking over the foodstuffs on the table, Owen shook his head. This was a ridiculous plan. There was no way he could accomplish it. But rather than let that defeat him, his determination grew. He would do this. For Dorothy.

He only had a few hours before she would be home from the Miller Ranch. So, he rolled up his sleeves and tied on Dorothy's apron. He had a cake to bake. Surely, that would show her how much she meant to him. After all, he had cooked on the trail before. How hard could this be?

He read the scrawled-out directions from her recipe book. The page had faded and crinkled with age. How long had it been in her book? For the most part, it seemed rather untouched. That didn't surprise him. She probably only looked at it the one time.

Mix sugar and butter into a cream.

Where? Should he put the butter into the sugar tin? Now, that didn't seem right. He only needed one cup of sugar.

There was more than that in the tin. Was he supposed to do it on the table? That would make a big mess. This was so different than anything he'd attempted. Chili was the most elaborate thing he made on the cattle trail. And that he had mixed in the cooking pot. Was he supposed to mix it all in the cake pans? He closed his eyes and tried to remember his wife baking. She usually had a bowl to put everything in.

So, he needed a bowl. Rummaging through the dish cabinet, he found one he thought suitable.

Now, for the cup of sugar. What kind of cup? He looked in the cabinet again. There were the drinking cups and the coffee mugs. The drinking cup must be it. Shoving the cup into the tin, he quickly realized he wasn't going to fill it that way. So, he set the cup on the table and dumped sugar from the tin.

It wasn't the cleanest way, he was certain, but it worked. He didn't think the half cup of butter would pour out the same way. Maybe a spoon would help. Adding the butter by spoon into the drinking glass worked. But it was a slow wait to dump the butter into the sugar, watching it slide down the side of the cup.

Something wasn't right about that. But it was the best he could figure.

The front door creaked. Owen's attention jerked in that direction. Who would be disturbing him? Was it Dorothy home early? He reached his arms around his things, hoping to hide them.

Eugene Hayworth's torso appeared around the door. "You home, Ow—"

Owen's face heated. Whether he should be embarrassed about his cooking adventure or not didn't have time to register.

"What in tarnation are you doing?" The man's voice was incredulous.

"What's it look like?" Owen stood straight once more. "I'm baking a cake."

Eugene's gaze flitted over the apron, the bowl, and the dusting of sugar on the table. "I see."

"Don't start with me. I'm doing this to surprise Dorothy."

Eugene stepped into the cabin and closed the door behind himself. "Oh?"

"Yeah. She had a hard day yesterday, and I want to show her how much I appreciate her. So, either get in here and help me or move on."

"Let's see if we can keep this a little less messy. It won't do any good to make her a cake and a big mess to clean up."

Owen looked around him and nodded.

Eugene moved next to him and picked up the recipe, his hands shaking as they always did.

"Maybe you can read the directions, and I'll add the stuff."

Eugene nodded, not taking his gaze from the paper. "I guess you've done the first step."

Glancing in the bowl, Owen grabbed for the spoon. "I've got to mix it."

Eugene watched him. What for? It made Owen a little uncomfortable.

"Well, go on. I'll wait."

Owen jumped slightly and stirred the sugar and clumps of butter together. But they didn't make the batter he often saw put into pans for cake making. Had he messed it up already?

"I think that'll do," Eugene said, putting a hand on Owen's and stilling him. "Next, you need to beat in the eggs."

Owen grabbed for two eggs, broke them, and got...well, most of the egg goo...into the bowl. Then he mixed some more.

"Good. Next, we need to add in two teaspoons of vanilla."

Owen did his best to pour the dark liquid over his mixing

spoon and into the forming batter, but he spilled more than he'd liked into the barely blended ingredients.

"That's okay," Eugene piped in. "Most folks like vanilla. It's sweet."

"What's next?"

"Two cups of flour."

The men worked tirelessly until they were, at last, ready to put the batter-filled pans into the oven.

"Are you sure it's supposed to be so lumpy?" Owen asked, pausing to look at the concoction before shoving it in.

"It's fine, I tell you. Put them pans in."

Owen set the pans in the oven and shut the door. "Only time will tell, I suppose."

"Trust me, it's going to be great." Eugene didn't seem as certain as Owen would have liked. Especially as he scanned the kitchen. "That's a lot of flour."

Indeed, the white powder had seemed to cover everything —including him and Eugene. What would Dorothy think of this mess?

"We'd best clean this up," he told Eugene.

His friend appeared more uncertain. "Where do we start?"

Owen looked around. Where indeed? So, he shrugged.

"You know what..." Eugene inserted. "She won't be home for a couple of hours. Why don't we sit for a piece?"

Owen's hip had started hurting something fierce. As much as he wanted to get the cleaning done first, his body's protests won out. And he nodded.

Then he and Eugene all but fell into the armchairs by the fire. Silence came over them as Owen considered the work they'd put in. It wasn't long before he closed his eyes. Just for a moment.

"What in the world?" a loud shriek drove Owen from his sleep.

What was going on? What had happened? He jerked to awareness, ready to face down whatever it might be.

Well, almost. He was not prepared to see his wife standing just within the doorway, eyes wide, and fanning air away from her face.

What?

Then it returned. He glanced down at his flour-covered clothes and apron. The mess. They had not cleaned up the mess. But there was more. A stench had filled the cabin. Like the smell of burned food.

Oh, no!

He rose, his intention to rush to the oven. But Dorothy was already halfway there.

Still, he moved toward the kitchen as she opened the oven door. Smoke rolled out and into her face. Without a word, she reached in with a towel and pulled out the smoldering cake pans.

As he watched her start to remedy the immediate situation and then wave her towel around the kitchen to push the smoke toward the door, his heart dropped. His plan...his desire to show her kindness and love...was ruined.

His eyes watered. From the smoke or from his emotion? He didn't wait to decide before picking up another towel and assisting his wife.

After the smoke cleared for the most part, she turned on him. "Are you all right?"

He nodded, somewhat sheepishly.

"What happened here?" Hands on hips, she scanned the surfaces in her kitchen and dining area.

He tried to push out words, but they couldn't pass over the lump in his throat.

She stepped to the pans and examined them. "Did you try to make something?"

He nodded. "A cake."

"A cake?" Her eyes widened again. "Whatever for? If you wanted a cake, I could have..." Something flashed in Dorothy's eyes.

"I can explain."

She didn't seem to hear him as she looked over the house, as if with new eyes. "You did this for me?"

It was both a question and a statement. She knew.

He nodded again, dropping his regard to the floor.

Someone moved beside him. He glanced at his likewise floured friend and looked back to his wife. "We did."

Eugene poked him.

"It was my idea, though." Owen fessed up.

Dorothy finished her scrutiny of the area, and her gaze once more landed on Owen. "That is just the sweetest..." Her words faded as her body jerked. Then laughter bubbled from her. She thought this was funny? Was that possible?

As he watched her laughter intensify to the point her eyes watered, the same levity overtook him. Soon they were both howling.

"You two are a sight," she managed as she sighed.

Owen nodded, knowing it was true. "We'll clean it all up."

She stepped to him, placing a kiss on his lips. "*We* will clean it up."

"But—"

Pressing her fingers to his mouth, she said, "Nonsense. If I want my kitchen back in order, I'm going to have to help."

He nodded. She was right. Who knew what further disaster he and Eugene might make of her space?

Together, they all set to work.

Owen eased into the bed at last. It had been a long day. One of the longest and most tiring of recent memory. Kitchen work was difficult. Much more so than he'd ever given his wife credit for.

Dorothy entered the room, her nightdress already on. "Everything is back in its place."

He nodded, wanting to apologize again but not sure how that would come across.

She settled into their bed, letting out a sigh as her body released its tension into the mattress. Then she turned to him. "Thank you."

What? She was thanking him? For messing up her kitchen? Burning her cake? Ruining her evening? His features must have betrayed his confusion.

She continued, "I needed that laughter. More than I needed a cake."

He thought on her words but wasn't certain what to say.

"These days, my feelings seem to be all over the place. One minute I'm happy, the next I can't stop crying."

Dare he mention that he had noticed? No. Best to just let her talk.

"And I have had more of the crying than the happiness these last several days. But you reminded me how important it is to see the humor in things. To laugh."

He nodded, wishing that had been his intention. Rather than a complete accident.

She set a hand to the side of his face. "You always do know just what I need. Whether you mean it or not."

How was it that she could always read him so well? He pressed a kiss to her palm. "You do so much for me. And for everyone else. I wanted to do something for you."

"I know." She smiled, her eyes twinkling in the moonlight.

"And you did. Not that I want to clean my kitchen like this every night, but maybe I should have more days like this—with more fun and lightness to them."

"I think I can help with that part." He grinned.

"I know you can."

As they nestled closer together, the worries of the past days melted away, and they rested in their love for each other.

May

GOLDEN YEARS

Dorothy waved her hand to cool the burning sensation from it. She knew better than to pour without looking. A mastered task, it still did not mean that she never erred. As evidenced by a hand with heated skin from spilled coffee. She just hoped that Owen wouldn't catch wind of it. The man could be insufferable. Even if he was darling while doing so.

"Everything set for Slim and Ada's wedding?" Dorothy wiped at the remainder of the spill on the counter.

"Hmm?" Amanda sat at the dinner table. And she seemed rather distracted. "Oh...Ada and Slim...yes, everything is ready. We'll be leaving for Tombstone later this week."

"It might be nice to get away for a bit." Dorothy smiled at the younger woman. But Amanda didn't even look her way. "Something bothering you, dear?"

"I just don't know what to think, Cook," Amanda said from the dinner table. "Brandon and I had...words."

Dorothy picked up the two freshly poured cups of coffee and brought them to the table. Sliding one in front of Amanda, Dorothy took a seat next to her. A glance in the

67

direction Amanda's gaze was set found Dorothy face-to-face with the big brown eyes of little Oliver. Mobile now, it had become difficult to keep him in one spot for any length of time.

How on earth did Amanda do it? These youngins required so much energy. But that wasn't what Amanda needed today. She and that husband of hers had crossed hairs.

"You've known Brandon a long time," Amanda said. "Why is he so stubborn?"

Dorothy couldn't hold back a small laugh. Brandon was just like his Uncle Owen. Apple doesn't fall far from the tree.

Amanda quirked an eyebrow.

"It's not you, dear." Dorothy reached out and put a hand on Amanda's forearm. "I can well relate. My Owen is just the same."

Amanda's eyebrow dropped, but the smile Dorothy expected to appear, did not. She must truly be upset.

"These men don't mean to be difficult. I have to believe that. They have their way of thinking, and it's not easy for them to get used to a woman having better ideas." She winked.

Amanda sighed. "Sometimes, I think we make progress in this area. But other times, like yesterday, I'm not so sure. Brandon sure does know his mind. Wish he knew mine a little better."

"Oh, posh!" Dorothy muttered.

"Pardon?" Amanda's eyes widened.

"You would be bored to tears if he had you all figured out. And I can't imagine how stifling that would be. Some of the sweetest things in marriage are our differences...and the friction."

"Why, Cook! Look who's turned into a romantic!"

Dorothy smiled and settled back into her chair as she raised her mug to her lips. When she lowered her arm again, she found Amanda's gaze on her, pensive, thoughtful.

"Is there something on my face?" Dorothy wiped at her mouth.

Amanda shook her head. Then, after a brief pause, she leaned in. "Can I be honest about something?"

"Land sakes, child, I hope you are being honest all the time."

Amanda's mouth tilted upward on one side. "Always." She looked down at her cup. "I mean...can we talk frankly?"

Whatever could Amanda want to share? Dorothy swallowed her trepidation and nodded, gripping her mug a bit too snuggly.

"Well...when things get...heated...with Brandon and me. It gets him all...stirred up. If you know what I mean?"

Of course, Dorothy knew what she meant. The deepening color on Amanda's face was enough to give it away, even if she hadn't. Dorothy bit her lip to keep from laughing out loud. "You know, dear, sometimes that helps."

Amanda's lips widened then as she hunched over. "Do you ever have trouble finding the...inspiration...just after being angry?"

"Sometimes." Dorothy thought it best to return Amanda's honesty. Besides, it was just between them.

"How do you...?" Amanda seemed to struggle to find the word she wanted.

"Soldier on?" Dorothy offered, trying to stifle a giggle.

Amanda's eyes most certainly couldn't get any wider. If they did, she was in real danger of them falling right out of her head.

"Now, now..." Dorothy was losing her battle to maintain a straight face. "That can be a problem indeed." She sipped her coffee as if they had all the time in the world.

"Well?" came Amanda's rather harsh whisper.

Dorothy's laughter faded, but her smile didn't. "I made a decision years ago when my sister and I had a similar conversation. And, though I didn't know who—or even if—God would bring me for a husband, I started praying."

Amanda watched Dorothy with rapt attention. But a curiosity flitted across her eyes. Yes, she wanted Dorothy to get to the answer she sought.

"I prayed not only for my husband, but that I would always be able to...respond to his touch." Now, it was Dorothy's turn for her face to heat.

"Oh?" Amanda swallowed, but her lips lifted.

The door slammed off to the left.

Dorothy froze. Who had heard? She turned her head slowly. It was as if time itself had started to stop.

And there stood Owen. An amused look directed right at her.

Dorothy's face was on fire. What had she said? What had he heard? He just stood there...smiling like the cat who ate the canary.

"I've got to change Oliver." Amanda's abrupt words cut through Dorothy's frantic thoughts.

The younger woman scooped up her son, threw Dorothy an apologetic look, and dashed from the room as if escaping a fire.

Why hadn't they heard the door open? Had someone recently oiled the hinges? She became desperate to speak but was unable to make her mouth move.

"What was all that about?" Owen asked, a smirk still on his face.

To play innocent? Or face the music? Dorothy struggled for the right choice.

"Whatever do you mean?" She took a quick sip of coffee, hoping against hope that he would not push.

When she lowered the mug, Owen's curious gaze was set on her. "Amanda leaving like that. Are you two up to something?"

Dorothy stood and grabbed for Amanda's mug. "I can't imagine what you mean. Oliver needed changing." She turned and moved into the kitchen.

To her chagrin, she heard the clomping of Owen's uneven steps coming after her.

"That ain't all," he called as he neared.

Keeping her back to him, she pumped water into the sink. "Oh, you just never mind our chatter. It's nothing to concern yourself with." Could her cheeks sustain any more heat? She doubted it. And she prayed that he wouldn't make her face him. There was little doubt she could disguise such bright red.

"No...I know when there's something up, and for sure you're hiding something." His demeanor was light, but his words carried a more serious tone.

"It's nothing. Really. Just some idle chitchat." She tried to wave him off.

"Oh? Seems like you were talking about me."

"Now, Owen, vanity does not suit you." She tried to force some strength into her own tone. But fell pitifully short.

His hand landed on her shoulder, and he urged her to turn. She resisted for a moment, but it was useless. However, that didn't mean she had to meet his gaze.

"I declare, Mrs. Miller. You sure are a sight." He chuckled.

That lit a fire in her belly. And she jerked her chin up. "As if you're so—"

He held up a hand. "Now, don't go blowing steam at me. Is that the way you want to 'respond to my touch'?"

She inhaled sharply. So, he had heard. He had nerve. "I need to check the laundry." Whirling around, she ignored his protests and all but ran out of the homestead.

Dorothy made sure Owen didn't catch her alone for the remainder of the day. After supper, however, she would have no choice but to load up in the wagon and face the ride home.

Amanda came up behind her as they were finishing in the kitchen, sliding a hand into hers. "Thanks for the talk," she whispered.

"Anytime." Her voice wavered, but she couldn't do anything about that. How could she disguise that she was more than a little uneasy about the upcoming hours alone with her husband and his judgments?

"Sorry we got interrupted." Amanda's gaze found a home on the floorboards. "I hope Uncle Owen didn't hear..." She swallowed.

"Don't you think on it one more moment." Dorothy set her hands on Amanda's shoulders. "Everything is right as rain."

"Even better." Amanda grinned as she blushed. "Brandon snuck inside before supper and we talked."

"That's wonderful."

Amanda's reddening features gave her away.

"Oh, is that how it was?" Dorothy relished a moment in which she wasn't focused on herself but could celebrate with her dear friend. "Glad to hear it."

Amanda sighed and met Dorothy's gaze. She really was moonstruck...so in love with that husband of hers.

Just then, the floorboards in the hall squeaked. Moments later, Brandon popped his head into the room. "I, um, was hoping to speak with you about something."

Dorothy turned away so Brandon wouldn't catch her stifling a laugh. The situation was uncomfortable enough as it was.

"Be right there," Amanda's voice was soft and a little lower than normal. "I just need to finish up in here with—"

"I think we've got everything." Dorothy beamed at the two of them. "Go on. I'll see myself out."

Amanda squeezed Dorothy's hand and moved off toward her husband. The two disappeared into the hallway, and Dorothy's shoulders shook. But she kept her laughter quiet.

It wasn't long before the front door opened. Oh, *now* she heard it. The devil was at work here.

"Ready?" Owen stood just inside the homestead.

"In a minute."

"Where did everyone go?" He looked around the dining room and peered into the kitchen.

"The ranch hands are bunked. The children are tucked in. And Brandon and Amanda are...enjoying some privacy."

"I see." There was a twinkle in his eye. He opened his mouth as if to say something but stopped himself.

"Go on and hitch old Bessie. I'll be out in a minute."

He nodded and stepped back outside.

Dorothy took in a deep breath and let it out. *Dearest Lord, help me to have a greater desire for peace with my husband. More than my rathers to defend my pride.*

Dorothy could sense Owen tossing glances her way. They had not been in the wagon ten minutes yet, and she couldn't stand it. How long could she hold out? This tension, as it was, grated on her. Why couldn't she just tell Owen the truth and let things fall where they may?

But she couldn't make herself speak first. So, silence it was.

The rest of the ride passed slowly. By the time they pulled onto their property, she had about cracked under the pressure. Now that they were home, maybe she could rush through her nighttime routine and be in the bed before Owen could ask after the happenings at the Miller Ranch.

When he stopped the cart, she worked her way down. And, as she turned, found him just behind her. Jerking back, she set a hand over her heart. "Owen Miller, you gave me a fright!"

"A fright, huh?" He was so close. How did he get out of the wagon so quickly? "Am I so scary?" His voice had deepened.

She gathered her nerve and swatted at his shoulder. "I've got things to tend to." Why wouldn't she just admit her embarrassment and let things work themselves out? Her husband was a good man. But he did have that humor-loving streak in him. And she didn't think any of this was funny.

Trying to move around him, she soon found herself pinned by his arms on either side of her. She tilted her head to the ground, denying him her face. "What do you think you are doing?"

He tipped her face toward him with a finger on her chin. "I think you know."

She sighed.

"Aw, come on, Dorothy, is it so bad?"

Her gaze clashed with his. "What?" Why would she continue to play this game?

"That I overheard what you said."

She shifted her focus to look at the cabin over his shoulder. "No. I just..."

"What?"

Remembering her prayer, she swallowed. And gathered all the gumption she had to force out the truth. "I was a bit embarrassed."

"Embarrassed?" He leaned away, giving her some space. "It's just me."

"Well, yeah. But I care about what you think." A weight lifted as she spoke those words.

"Shoot, Dorothy. I'm your husband. There's no reason to let a little embarrassment stick between us. How many times have I got myself in a fix that I should've known better about?"

He had a point there. The man did have a penchant for trouble. And he hadn't let any shame he felt get in the way.

"I didn't mean to tease you so." His voice was gentle. "I just...got all soft at your words."

She met his gaze again. "Oh?"

"Yeah. You prayed for me? All those years? And then you prayed that you would..." His voice trailed as he ran a hand down her arm. It was his turn to swallow hard.

She offered him a small smile. "Well, yeah. I love you. I don't ever want to pull back when you need tenderness."

He arched a brow. "Like you did today?"

That was true. She might have prayed that she'd respond to his touch, but she had not been faithful to lean into him in the midst of conflict.

She let out a long breath. "Like I did today."

His lips quirked on one side.

"You sure are handsome when you do that."

Beaming wider, his face seemed to light up.

Lifting onto her tiptoes, she pressed her lips to his. Arms wrapped around her and drew her close. When they parted, he touched his mouth to the tip of her nose. "Now, that's more like it."

June

WORTH IT'S WEIGHT IN GOLD

Owen Miller struggled through the front door of the cabin he shared with his wife. That old hip—the one injured so long ago—had bothered him something fierce today. More than it had in several weeks. Working his way into the small house with shuffling, uneven steps, he managed to make it to a chair at the dining table. Not the most comfortable seat, but he doubted he could've taken the extra steps required to get to his armchair.

He settled in as best he could and rubbed the offended joint. As if that would do anything. No one, not even the doctor, had given him advice that helped. Except, of course, to rest and stay off of it. But that only seemed to make the leg stiffer, more difficult to move.

Though he may not have a choice at this point.

Minutes passed as he sat, shifting his body this way and that in an attempt to take pressure off the hip. It was no use. But in time, the aching throb gentled, and he leaned back, closing his eyes and offering a prayer of gratitude.

His mind wavered in that space between prayer and drifting into sleep when he heard hoofbeats. Twisting to get a view out of the window, he was rewarded with a fresh stab of pain through the old injury. He grimaced. Would he never learn?

Helpless, he could do nothing but listen and wait.

The hoofbeats drew near and then stopped just outside. Booted feet thudded on the porch steps. And, finally, a knock sounded on the door.

"Who is it?" he pressed out through clenched teeth, hoping his words didn't betray his debility

"It's Eugene."

Owen breathed out his relief. He might not want his friend to know of his distress, but he could trust the man even if he did see. "Come in."

The door opened slowly, and Eugene stepped into the cabin. "Owen?"

"Over here," he called.

Eugene scanned the area, squinting as his eyes adjusted to the slightly dimmer area. "Where are y—?"

Owen did what he could to mask his discomfort just as Eugene's gaze landed on him.

"You okay?"

Perhaps he hadn't disguised it so well after all. "I'm fine. Just my hip giving me fits again."

Eugene's brows furrowed. But he didn't speak of it further. He moved into the house, shutting the door, and crossing to where Owen sat. As Eugene took the seat next to Owen, he laid a hand on the tabletop. He held a telegram; it shook as his arm trembled. But Owen knew better than to think it due to the contents of the message. The man had long since had these tremors throughout his arms and hands. It caused Owen more than a little concern.

Owen locked eyes with his friend. "You got word? From Missy? Or one of your boys?"

Eugene's daughter was the one who wrote most often, but

she wasn't apt to send telegrams. Was there some urgent need for her to do so?

The man nodded. He seemed to hunt for his words. Was he so flustered? "It's from Dan."

Dan? Had something happened? Owen's nerves bristled. *Dear God, not Lily or the baby!*

"It's a boy," Eugene let out on a breath. "I have a grandson."

Something still seemed unsettled about the man.

"How is Lily?" Owen was almost afraid to ask.

Eugene looked to the paper. Did he not want to say? Perhaps, he only needed to reread the details. When he looked up again, a smile played at his mouth, and Owen could breathe again.

"She is well."

"Praise the Lord!" Owen took a moment to thank God for His protection of the dear woman who had become like a daughter to Owen.

Eugene nodded. "There's not much here beyond the announcement. Only..."

"Only what?"

"His name." Eugene's Adam's apple bobbed in response, and he cleared his throat as he looked away. What would cause such a reaction?

"Well?"

"Gene Owen Hayworth."

Well...that was something else. Dan and Lily named the baby after his grandfather and the man not truly blood related to either of them.

"It's a good name." Eugene's voice broke on the last word, and he seamed his lips.

"A strong name," Owen said. He couldn't help but note the slight shaking in his own voice.

"Just think," Eugene started. It was several moments

before he was able to continue. "Our names together in that little thing."

"I hope it does him proud." Owen again lifted a prayer, this time for the child and the life ahead of him.

"I imagine Dorothy will be tickled pink. If she doesn't already know."

Owen couldn't nail down what Eugene might mean. How would Dorothy know? Did Dan notify those at the Miller Ranch first? Before Eugene? Though that batch of fellas had always been close, he didn't think Dan would do so.

"Oh," Eugene said, as if he realized Owen's inability to connect everything. "I saw Dorothy at the General Store before I headed to collect my mail. I would wager that Dan sent word to you two also."

"Dorothy was in town?" Why wasn't she at the Miller Ranch? Perhaps, Eugene only thought he saw her.

Eugene tilted his head to the side. "And I might as well warn you. She was talking rather adamantly with Cleo Norris."

"Cleo Norris?" Of all the... Owen had known this day would come. He'd just hoped it wouldn't. At least, not during his lifetime. Dorothy would have a bushel of questions for him when she got home. Questions he would have to answer. It was high time he did.

Twenty-three-year-old Owen Miller was pleased to have passed Wharton City. It wouldn't be long before they arrived at Blanchard's Ranch. The thrill of all that awaited him coursed through his muscles. They would be off the trail, in actual beds, with some real food.

But that wasn't all. Cleo would be waiting.

He looked at his boss. The man didn't know about the

budding relationship between Owen and his daughter. And it needed to stay that way. Maybe this drive would change that. Owen had earned a good sum in these last months. Things that weren't possible before, might now be possible.

They slowed the horses as the ranch appeared on the horizon. Owen's heart skipped a beat before it thudded hard. Just the thought of his fair Cleo, and he pressed his horse to go a little faster.

The blond-haired beauty, curls barely contained by a ribbon, had been the object of his affection since he came out west to escape his family. And her visage had been the vision before him every waking moment since departing the ranch near a month ago.

He'd never imagined that this opportunity to work the drive would lead to a desire to stay. But he had already talked with Blanchard about a more permanent arrangement at the ranch. He'd be able to see Cleo every day.

The hard work didn't matter to Owen. It seemed as nothing in light of time spent with Cleo. No matter that as the son of a prominent lawyer in Richmond he had never known difficult work. Or work with his hands at all, for that matter. But that life wasn't for him. Not anymore. He'd let his brother take on the family business. Charles was always the more settled between them anyway. The more...responsible one.

They reined in the horses as they neared the barn. When Owen dismounted, a hand landed on his shoulder. He turned. Jim Blanchard stood behind him.

"You did good."

"Thank you, sir." He held the man's gaze, determined not to show weakness.

"Stable the mares and take a load off."

Owen nodded before taking the reins from Blanchard and urging the animals into the barn and to their stalls. Taking off their saddles, brushing, feeding, and watering two horses took some time. And it wasn't long before he was the only one left.

Sighing, he moved to the far side to hang the bits and bridles.

"So, you're back." The voice was feminine. And it came from just behind him.

He turned to see his vision come to life. Cleo stood not two arms' lengths away. His mouth widened in a smile that fairly hurt his cheeks. "You knew I would be."

Her lips tilted upward. And she moved toward him.

He couldn't keep himself from gathering her in his arms and hugging her close.

"I missed you," she whispered. There was a touch of sadness in her voice. Why? Had she truly longed for him so much?

"Me, too," he managed, swallowing to keep his voice from betraying just how much.

She pulled away, but he caught her hands. Though she didn't resist, she looked down. Owen ignored the nagging in his head that warned something was wrong. Surely, she was just as overcome with emotion as he was.

"I've decided to stay. Here. On the ranch."

Her head shot up, and her eyes widened. "What?"

"I'm not going back to Richmond."

She looked off to the side. Was she avoiding him?

He tugged at her hands. "Did you hear me? I think I made enough to set up a small place for us."

Her gaze was on him again, but her features were sorrowful. Did she not understand?

"We can be married," he continued, as if everything in him were not screaming for prudence, for him to tread carefully.

"I...have something to tell you." Her words were bland. And her lips downturned, as if the words were as hard to speak as they would be to hear.

He nodded but couldn't make his mouth work.

"I'm engaged to Harold Norris."

No. It wasn't possible. Not after the things they'd said to each other. After what they meant to each other.

"But—" he started, the force of his words lacking as his strength failed him.

"Owen, I...didn't know. I didn't know you would stay."

"You mean, you didn't trust me."

"Harold has great plans to be something. And I just—"

"To be something? And I don't?"

"That's not what I meant." Her words were weak and pathetic. And the meaning behind them slammed into his gut. She thought he wasn't good enough.

"My parents think a lot of Harold, and my mother...she said—"

Owen cut her off. "Don't." He didn't need to hear anymore. Didn't want to hear anymore.

"I'm sorry." The words rang hollow as she pulled her hands free and backed away.

What was he going to do?

The door squealed, jarring Owen from his memories. But the sting remained. A heart spurned. A love thwarted.

Eugene gripped his arm. "You okay?"

Owen nodded, still shaking off the emotions that clung to him like molasses. He looked toward the door, but he knew who it was.

Dorothy moved into the house. She appeared a bit frazzled. And he didn't have to guess why. Though he might imagine the nature of her discussion with Cleo, he wondered at what exactly had been communicated. How much did Dorothy know?

"Hello, Eugene," she said, as she laid her few things on the table. "I suppose 'congratulations' are in order." A smile pressed onto her features. But there was more going on underneath. Owen could sense it.

"And to you and Owen," Eugene added. "I know Lily is dear to you two."

Dorothy nodded. Then she stepped farther into the kitchen. "It's just so wonderful. You fellas need some coffee?"

Owen cleared his throat. "Don't trouble yourself, now."

She met his gaze, her eyes pinning him. "It's no trouble at all."

When she turned back to the stovetop, he tossed a look at Eugene, who shrugged.

"You're home awful early," Eugene said, winking at Owen. Was the man trying to help somehow?

"Amanda insisted I leave. I needed to run an errand in town."

Eugene nodded, glancing between his friend and Dorothy as if he felt caught. This was no use.

Owen opened his mouth, but Dorothy cut him off. "Oh, and you'll never believe who I came across at the General Store."

Should he play dumb? That didn't seem right.

"The mayor's wife," Dorothy said in an almost sing-song way.

"Oh?" Owen put forth. So dumb it was.

Dorothy stopped her bustling and looked at him again. "She had some rather unkind words for me."

"Unkind?"

"Yes. And I wondered why she would all but attack me."

Owen let out a breath as he focused on the table.

"Then it hit me." Dorothy marched forward, coming that much closer to Owen and Eugene. "She had some kind of bone to pick with me. And you know what that was?"

Owen wanted to shake his head, but he couldn't keep up the act. He started to speak, but she cut him off again.

"Apparently, she has some idea that I've moved in on her territory."

Her territory? Cleo was a lot of things, but delusional was not one he'd suspected. True, she hadn't seemed happy when he and Dorothy married, but he'd never have thought she would clobber Dorothy these years later.

Eugene started to rise. "I think I'd best be on my way—"

"Sit," Dorothy commanded.

Eugene settled into his seat once more.

"Now, something is going on here, and one of you had best tell me."

Owen let out a breath. "It's nothing to get all worked up about. Cleo and me were sweethearts. Decades ago. And she decided to marry Harold Norris instead. Broke my heart."

Dorothy's mouth drooped open.

Eugene stared at the table.

"Sweethearts? And I'm just now hearing about this?" Dorothy did not seem relieved in the least by Owen's explanation.

"It was so long ago. I didn't think it was important."

"This is a woman of my acquaintance. A woman I see at church. A woman who cornered me today and gave me an earful. And you didn't think it was important?"

Why did she have to make such good sense? It made him look bad. Owen pursed his lips. "I didn't mean any harm. I figured she had made her decision, and I tried to forget the whole thing."

"Well, she may have made her bed, but she certainly don't like it, I tell ya."

Owen's eyes widened. What could that mean?

Dorothy shook a finger at him. "Now, don't you go

getting any ideas. You made your bed, too. Now you gotta lie in it."

"I think I'll get going," Eugene said again.

But Owen put a hand on his arm. As much as he hated for his friend to hear this, he needed some support. "Listen, Dorothy, that was a long time ago. Things have changed for me. I—"

"Have they?"

"How can you even ask that? I don't think of her that way. I love *you*. I married *you*."

Dorothy let out a long breath, and the tension released from her shoulders. "I guess I know that."

"You guess? How can you wonder?"

"She's just so different from me. How can you be sweet on her and then marry me?"

Owen shrugged. He had to find a way to further ease the situation. But he wanted to be honest with his wife. "Maybe I was too young to know what was good for me."

Dorothy's lips lifted. "I'm good for you?"

"Now, there's a silly question." He glanced at Eugene for confirmation, but the oaf just sat there and grimaced. Perhaps, all of this was making him uncomfortable.

She crossed to Owen and set her hands on either side of his face. "So, you don't wish you would have married her all those years ago?"

"Absolutely not. You are the right one for me." He wanted to stand and embrace her, but he doubted he'd be able to with his hip flaring up like it was .

It didn't matter, she leaned in and pressed a kiss to his mouth. "You do beat all."

He let his smile overtake his features.

"I can't stay mad at you, no matter how hard I try."

"Well, I'm not gonna argue with that," he eagerly agreed.

She laughed, and he joined in. He wrapped his arms around her, even seated, and tugged her closer.

"I...think I should go now." Eugene piped up, his voice strained.

Owen had forgotten that his friend sat nearby. His thoughts had been swirling around his wife.

Dorothy turned toward Eugene. "Nonsense. You stay for supper."

"I..." Eugene's gaze collided with Owen's.

"Stay. We'll be good." Owen winked at his wife.

She swatted at him. "You old charmer."

He turned her loose, and she moved back into the kitchen. Smiling at his friend, Owen let all the tension seep out of him. He was at home with his Dorothy. And he couldn't be more thankful for Cleo's rejection. The years that had followed that long ago moment had been lonely, but Dorothy had been worth the wait.

They were a match, all right.

Thank you, God, for prayers granted. And not.

July

AS PRECIOUS AS GOLD

Owen Miller pulled the reins to the right, angling the horse's movements in that direction. He wasn't often in Wharton City this past month, but he did find that there was a need to make this trip once a week for provisions and whatnot.

As usual, he would sneak something special for Dorothy into the wares. She scolded him every time, but her blush and the sweet smile that touched her lips insured he would repeat the gesture.

What would he find today?

He pulled the horse to a stop just in front of the General Store, and the mare came to a halt at his command. But he took a moment to stretch his leg out across the footrest.

Whatever could be done about this old hip? Nothing. Doc had mended what he'd been able to. Owen would have to get along with what ailment remained. No matter how he struggled. He hadn't much right to complain, though. Life had been good to him. A good woman and a fine nephew as a legacy. What more could he ask for?

But there was that ache. The one he would never breathe a

word to Dorothy about. His regrets that he'd never had a family of his own. It wasn't as if he didn't love Brandon as much as any son of his own flesh. Or that he would trade his relationship with the man for anything in the world. Still...

He shook his head. Such was the musings of an old man. Far past his youth, and long beyond the ability to have such notions as children of his own. It was nonsense. Utter nonsense.

Leaning to his left, he eased himself out of the wagon's seat. That was not a task he accomplished with grace, but he did reach solid ground without injury. For which he was thankful.

Breathing in air filled with the dust stirred by many horses and wheels traveling the main stretch, he coughed to clear his lungs. Ah, stuff and nonsense indeed. He'd best be done with his errands and return to the clearer air of the countryside. That's where he belonged.

A quick...well, slow walk to the postal office proved more fruitful than usual. There was a letter for Dorothy and one for him. The handwriting on his wife's letter was a giveaway. Her sister's regular correspondence had been reliable and was something Dorothy looked forward to. And his letter appeared to be from Brandon's sister. What might she have written to tell him?

Tucking the letters in his shirt pocket, he forced himself to save his for later. Dorothy would appreciate that. With the mail collected, his list for the General Store was all that remained. That...and Dorothy's something special...

Some time later, Owen directed the same cart and horse toward a very different destination. One that he was all too glad to see—the Miller Ranch. He would collect his darling

Dorothy on his way to their simple home. Only then, might he be able to find the rest due him after such a long day.

The homestead lay ahead, and he heard the dinner bell ringing loud and true. Would that be Samuel? What a fanciful thought! He hadn't been so enthralled with that task anymore. Not for a few years now. His attentions had been on...other things. More 'important' things.

Still, Owen was pleased to have arrived in time for the evening meal. But quite nearly too late. He pressed the horse to pick up step for the last several yards to the house.

Three figures strode from the barn. One would be his nephew. The man had done well for himself—a fine ranch and an even more remarkable family. It wasn't so long ago that Owen wondered if Brandon would resist God's offer of love and end up the bachelor Owen thought himself to be. But God had smiled down on both of them.

Brandon raised a hand toward Owen's cart as it neared and passed.

Owen lifted his hat and waved it at his much-loved nephew. Then he slowed the horse, bringing the mare to a stop by the porch.

And as he struggled out of the wagon, Brandon approached from around the back of the cart.

"Good to see you, Uncle Owen. You coming from town, I see."

Owen had just made it to the dirt-packed surface of the ground. Thankfully. He didn't relish the idea of Brandon seeing him work so hard, or worse—trying to help him.

Clapping a hand on Brandon's shoulder, he smiled at the younger man. "That's right."

Brandon nodded. "What'd you get for Cook this week?"

Was he so obvious? He knew he was. So, he returned his nephew's grin and held up a brown paper bag tied with a blue ribbon—Dorothy's favorite color. "Taffy."

"Well." Brandon put a hand to his stomach. "I hope Cook has a mind to share."

"Don't you so much as breathe a word to that, boy." Owen narrowed his gaze but quirked one brow to indicate he but jested.

Brandon flashed teeth with his broad smile. "Let's see what Cook has rustled up for dinner."

Owen let Brandon lead him into the house, where they found Amanda sitting at the table holding Oliver. The child cooed and babbled while grasping for his mother's long tresses.

Brandon stepped away from Owen and leaned over Amanda's shoulder to claim her lips.

Owen couldn't begrudge him; he understood the man's heart. As his own had been completely taken by his Dorothy. Which...where was she?

Clattering from the kitchen removed any doubt...as if there were need for any.

"You fellas seen that husband of mine? He best not let these taters get cold or I'll..." she said as she stepped into the dining room, her voice trailing off as she set eyes on him. "Well, look who decided to show up."

But he knew better than to be offended. Her eyes gleamed, and the corners of her mouth turned up as she set the pot of mashed potatoes on the table. She was glad to see him.

He took his hat off and put it to his chest. "As if I'd miss your homecooked meal."

She shook a hand at him as she moved back to the kitchen. "Pssha! You best wash up and take your seat."

"As the lady wishes." He turned toward Brandon and winked. "I'll be right back."

The gentle rocking of the wagon soothed Owen more than he'd have thought. Even as the vibration unsettled his hip. That old bum hip.

But Dorothy had moved a little closer to him and looped an arm through his, and that was all right with him.

Her other hand held the precious package with the blue ribbon.

"How is your taffy, my lady?"

"Oh, you just beat all, you know that? There is no good reason for you to buy me something every time you go to town."

"No?"

"No," she chided.

Silence cut between them as she adjusted the folds of her skirt.

"What if I was to say I disagree?"

Her head jerked up so fast he feared she may have hurt herself. "With what?"

"What if I say there *is* a good reason?"

"I suppose you want me to ask what that reason is." She let out a breath.

He leaned over, lowering his voice, as if he shared a great secret. In truth, he rather enjoyed their banter. "I say, I have good cause...as you're my girl."

Silence.

She didn't have anything to say?

A first, for sure.

She hugged his arm. "Oh, shoo! You sure know how to make a girl feel special."

"Just as long as I can make *my* girl feel special." He gave her a wink. And as he looked at her, he was certain he saw her cheeks color.

The bag crinkled as she held it tighter and brought that hand over to join the one around his arm.

"I almost forgot!" He jerked a little.

The horse startled. Had his motion been so great that he had pulled on the reins?

Her eyes were on his.

He reached into his shirt pocket. "We each got a letter."

Her hand opened and received the precious envelopes. She gazed at the writing. These letters—ties to their loved ones—were precious indeed.

"Oh, Esther's letter. It has been a little delayed. I'd started to worry."

Delayed? He hadn't noticed. But leave it to Dorothy to take note of something like that.

"And Ada has written. How exciting! I do wish we could have shared it with Brandon."

"Maybe it's best we didn't. Not everything needs to be shared, you know."

She nodded.

It wasn't often, but at times, Ada confided in her uncle. And he knew she expected him to keep such things to himself. But certainly not from Dorothy.

"Oh, I'm just plum brimming with curiosity! What could it say?"

Owen peered over. Dorothy stared at the envelope bearing her sister's letter again. "It's still light out. Why don't you open it?"

She looked at him. Often, they saved these things until they could read them together in the great room. But her eyes were so wide and pleading.

He chuckled. "I mean it. Go ahead."

Dorothy needed no further prompting. She tore open the flap and pored over the page, flipped it over, and continued.

Then she stopped and laid a hand to his arm. "Oh my."

"What is it?" He didn't know if he should be concerned or upset or curious.

"She's coming for a visit." Dorothy's gaze met Owen's. Her eyes danced in the fading sunlight. Then she turned back to the letter. "Well, I never in a hundred years..."

"A visit?"

"Yes! And this letter must have been misdirected. She says she'll be here mid-July."

"Isn't that next week?"

Dorothy's eyes went wide. "As I live and breathe."

Owen put a hand on hers. "I'm sure everything will be fine."

She jerked her hand away. "You don't understand. I've got to...and then, I'll need...oh, it's just going to be..." Her breaths came in heaves.

"Calm down now. You won't solve anything by working yourself into a tizzy."

Her focus on him narrowed. "A what?"

He swallowed. "Now, I didn't mean that you—"

"Owen Miller, I do not...and I repeat, do *not* work myself into a tizzy. I never have, and I never will."

He clamped his mouth shut and faced forward. Was it his imagination or did the temperature in the whole of Arizona raise several degrees?

"I am simply...*concerned*...is all."

He licked his lips. What to say? So, he offered what he thought would be safe. "Of course."

Still glaring at him, she crossed her arms. Though he didn't dare look at her, he felt the intensity of her eyes boring into him.

Was she waiting on something else from him? He hoped not. Because there wasn't a chance in this century he was opening his mouth for the remainder of the ride home. Even if he sweat out most of his bodily fluids.

At length, she sighed. "There is much to do."

What was he in for?

Owen did his best to stay out of Dorothy's way. She was in a state this morning. Had been for the last two days. Would it ever stop? Perhaps, when her sister's coach arrived in a couple of hours, things would ease in the home.

Perhaps.

Who was he kidding?

Dorothy moved this way and that, cleaning and tidying things that had been cleaned and tidied more times than he could remember.

If only he might take her mind off these things. There couldn't be more preparations to make. At least, not any that mattered.

"How about we make our way toward town? Maybe meander through the General Store?"

The look she shot his way made him duck.

As he lifted his head, ever so cautiously, he caught her gaze, still intent on his figure.

"I only meant it might be..." He swallowed. "...nice to have a minute to relax before—"

"Relax? I haven't the time for such a thing. Don't you see I have to..." She looked around the space, cloth in hand on her hip. "And then I have to..."

In a bold move, Owen stood and stepped toward her. "If you care for my say at all—"

Another sharp look shot at him.

It was almost enough to halt him where he stood.

But not quite. He was determined she needed to stop all this. She had worked herself into a state! "The house has never looked better. You, my dear, have not let a detail slip through."

"But—" She held up her hands as she turned away, as if searching for an excuse.

Owen set a hand to her arm. "No 'buts.' You have worked hard enough. Everything is as ready as it will be."

Her dark eyes met his. Something passed in them. Sadness? Pleading? It was difficult to discern. He was more convinced than ever she needed some fresh air.

"Let's get your cleaning things put away." He lifted the cloth from her hand as he reached around with yet another streak of boldness and untied her apron.

To his surprise, there was no more protest from her. Just a deep sigh.

"I suppose you are right. Even if I work my fingers raw, it is what it is."

At that, he left the apron and lifted her hand to his lips and kissed her fingertips. "There now, let's have no more of that. 'Sides, I like your fingers just as they are." His mouth spread wide.

Her lips turned up in an attempt at a smile, but it still concerned him. Why was she so anxious about her sister's visit?

He hadn't had the pleasure to meet the woman, yet. But he had heard much about her through the exchanged letters. The woman seemed fine enough. And if she was well liked by his Dorothy, she couldn't be half bad. Dorothy was an excellent judge of character.

Although...it wouldn't be the first time someone had been blind where a family member or loved one was concerned.

He pushed that thought to the side and strengthened his smile once more.

Dorothy set her dirtied cloth to be laundered and hung her apron. Now she smoothed her hair into place. She needn't bother—it looked tucked up as good as ever to him. The woman always paid careful attention to her appearance. Though, if it were up to him, he'd prefer her with her hair down—silken strands falling loose around her shoulders. But that was a treat for him alone.

"What are you about?" Her voice cut through his thoughts.

His smile deepened. "Just thinkin' is all."

She narrowed her eyes. "Sounds like trouble to me."

He chuckled. "Let's get on to town."

Though her features still betrayed her suspicions, she allowed him to lead her outside and to the cart.

Owen had not released Dorothy's arm, though they now stood on the planked platform awaiting the stagecoach. And he noticed, she wasn't quick to pull away either. He enjoyed having her so close.

Patting her hand resting on his forearm, he looked at her.

She watched the horizon. The lines in her face had become more visible. Was she so concerned? Had his distraction not been sufficient?

And he wondered again...what was this that her sister held over her? Or did Dorothy work herself up for some reason that was within her?

He would have to figure it out as things unfolded. It was doubtful such a conversation would get him anything but another evil eye. And he didn't wish to distress her any more than she already was. He hated to see her so. Was there any way to ease her burden?

She shifted beside him and moved as if to pull away.

He held her more firmly, and she stilled. But he also looked in the direction where she focused.

There, surrounded by a cloud of dust, was the rocking and bouncing stagecoach, coming faster than could be safe. Still, the driver urged the horses onward, only slowing them as they came within a few feet of the town. By then, it seemed a bit late for that. The driver's lack of consideration for the comfort of his passengers was appalling. Those within would have certainly been jerked about at the quick change in speed.

The dust kicked up by the driver's inconsiderate maneuvering left Owen coughing. No doubt he and Dorothy, and everyone else waiting nearby, would be covered in it.

But the stage had arrived. At last, there was hope for this craziness in his wife and home to stop.

Owen watched as the young kid, much too young to be handling such an important task as being responsible for the safety of others, stepped down from the driver's seat. He then opened the small door and stuck a hand in to help the few passengers out.

Dorothy gasped.

He looked at her.

She seemed a bit winded. Had she been holding her breath?

He patted her hand again. "I'll go receive Esther."

Moving closer to the stage, Owen came up behind the driver and waited for a woman about Dorothy's age to be helped out. And he hoped there would be just the one on the stage. He hadn't met her. What if he made a fool of himself and collected the wrong woman?

First a younger, red-haired woman stepped out of the coach. An older woman behind Owen called to her. Then a boy, who couldn't have been more than ten years old, exited. The driver indicated that he should wait by the telegraph office.

Then a raised voice from within fussed at the driver.

Owen smiled. That woman had to be Dorothy's kin.

The driver shook his head and wiped perspiration from his forehead but then stepped up and reached in. Soon enough, he backed out of the coach, his hand steadying the woman emerging.

And then Dorothy came out of the coach.

Owen's heart stopped for a moment.

He looked back at the platform. Yes, she was still there. Then how was she being helped out of the coach?

Was her sister her...were they...could it be...the sisters were *twins*?

Owen held the door open for the two sisters to enter the small cabin, though if they noticed him, he would have been surprised. They chattered on just as they had since the two had been face-to-face upon Esther's arrival .

And what a dizzying experience that had been for him. Why hadn't Dorothy bothered to tell him Esther was her twin? Had it simply been an oversight or did Dorothy keep that to herself on purpose? If so, why?

He smiled as the women passed by him.

They were rather animated. Best he could tell, Esther still complained about the coach ride. Not that he blamed her. The driver had seemed rather fool hardy.

Owen was relieved when he closed the door behind them, creating a sound barrier that only muffled the ongoing conversation.

He let out a breath. What would the next weeks bring? Glancing heavenward, he sent up a prayer that something might call the woman home sooner than expected. Was that so awful? It was difficult to care as he walked back to the cart, his ears still ringing from the constant assault.

Grabbing for the mare's bit, he led her toward the barn then went about stabling her and making sure she was refreshed and fed. Yes, he needed to tend to the animal—it wasn't just that he dallied, avoiding the overly wordy company of his sister-in-law—but he had to admit that it was part of it.

As time passed, his reason for delaying his return to the house thinned. He would have to return, or Dorothy would have his hide.

He entered the house, and Esther's voice filled his senses. Had she not let up at all? Did Dorothy get an opportunity to say anything?

Glancing at his wife, he offered her a smile. Was she just as caught by her sister's verbose ways?

But Dorothy did not look in his direction. She seemed intent on her hands in her lap when she wasn't giving some menial response to Esther.

For all intents and purposes, Esther ignored Owen. He was not put off though and moved toward the sink's water pump to wash up.

Only then did he catch bits of their conversation.

"My John is doing just as well as you can imagine. Has the prettiest wife in all of Alabama. And he is running for mayor of Lewisburg. I'm just proud as can be. They'll be busy, though, come early spring. He'll be a father!

"And Darlene! That girl is turning every head in Tuscaloosa! I have a mind she'll be engaged before the year is out. This will be her last year teaching for certain."

Esther's monologue continued on, but Owen became more and more confused. Hadn't Esther's eldest, Thomas, written Dorothy that John had found himself on the wrong side of the law not two months ago? And that Darlene had been struggling to get adjusted and make friends?

Why would she let her sister continue on with such a display? Esther put on in such a way that could only be meant to show up her poor sister, who didn't have even one child to boast over?

He looked at his wife. No, she had great restraint and grace for her sister. But he couldn't abide watching Dorothy sit and take this any longer.

"Esther," he broke in, cutting her off midsentence.

She turned to look at him, her eyes widened. Was she so horrified that he would dare?

"You must be something awful tired from your trip."

"I'm not as—"

"Especially after that terrible, unbearable jostling of the stagecoach and all. I can't imagine what you've been through."

"I suppose..."

He moved closer to where she sat. "Absolutely. Please, don't let us keep you from taking time to rest from such an ordeal."

"Well, I—"

He held out an arm. "Dorothy has fixed up a nice place for you just this way." Reaching for Esther's arm in a bold move, he assisted her to her feet and ushered her toward the sectioned-off area they had prepared for her.

Owen felt Esther's muscles tense, but she didn't make any other move to resist him.

The sooner he could settle her out of sight...and earshot... for a few moments, the better.

Owen returned to the great room and found that Dorothy's chair had been vacated. A few quick steps into the kitchen left him in equal surprise that it, too, was empty.

Where could she have gone? And why?

Glancing around the cabin, a flash of silver outside, through the window, caught his eye. Had she stepped out? For fresh air, perhaps? Or respite?

He made short work of hobbling to the door and out to where she stood, gazing toward the horizon.

As he came up beside her, he heaved for some moments. And so they remained in silence. She didn't bother to ask him why he interrupted her and her sister's reunion, or why he followed her outside. But as the minutes ticked by, he reached the end of his tolerance. Yet, he sensed it was best to approach this slow and easy.

"Want to talk about it?"

She sighed, never taking her eyes off the place where the sky met the earth.

"Not the answer I was looking for."

Rather than push further, he let his gaze drift over the landscape. It was peaceful. But this whole thing had become a bit odd. His Dorothy was the last to be a wallflower. And now, silent and thoughtful? It wasn't right.

"I don't know what to say." Her words surprised him when they came. He had given up expecting her to speak.

"Oh, you know you can tell me anything. I'm always—"

"To *her*." Now, she met his gaze. Her eyes were sad and hard at the same time. "I don't know what to say to *her*."

Owen nodded. He'd rarely known Dorothy to be bereft of speech. What was it about her sister that brought this about? Moreover, how was he to encourage her?

"I'm sure proud you didn't let her goad you. I know she was fibbin' about a lot of what she said."

Dorothy's brows rose.

"About her kids."

She turned to look back at the scenery. "Maybe she didn't. Maybe they don't tell her what's what."

He hadn't considered that. Perhaps, that was true. That still didn't explain why Dorothy would let her sister brag and throw it all in her face.

"I'm still glad you can find it in your heart to stay at peace."

Her eyes fell on his again.

He turned to face her, settling an arm around her shoulders. "I know that can't be easy with all she says."

Dorothy's brows furrowed.

"You know, talking up her kids. As if she thinks to indicate that you..." His words trailed. Now, he was the villain. He was the one pointing out that she was childless. Opening a wound he knew little about.

Her gaze fell.

"I'm sorry." He wanted to kick himself. But it wasn't about him. It was about her. "I didn't mean to."

When Dorothy lifted her eyes again, they were full of emotion...such that it was difficult for him to discern what she felt.

"I don't think she means it. That's just all she knows."

What could she mean by that?

"Our mother always compared us. It's just natural for her to continue to do so."

"That don't make it right."

"Doesn't it?" Dorothy's eyes glistened. Would there be tears?

"Your life is different from hers. Your path went a different way."

Dorothy nodded. "Maybe it was my own fault, though."

He furrowed his brows.

"Wasn't it my fault I stopped living when Harry died?"

Her fiancé. The one lost in the War Between the States.

"Don't say such things. You managed. You did what you could."

"Did I? How is it anyone else's fault that I shut every other man out of my life until I was a spinster? An old maid? Well beyond my viable years?" Her voice trembled with pain that clearly remained after all these years.

"Listen to me. No one can know what will come.

Everyone can look back and see what we could have done better."

She watched him. Was she disbelieving of his words?

"But *God.*"

"What?"

"God changed your story. And He changed mine. Forever. When I met you."

A tear slipped down the side of her face.

Owen moved closer. "And I wouldn't have my story any other way."

She pressed into him. And he wrapped his arms around her. Her body shook, and he felt moisture collecting on his shirt. But he didn't mind one bit. For he had spoken true. God had blessed him, indeed. He needed her.

And she him.

To have and to hold.

Yet again, they were at the stagecoach platform. Owen watched as Dorothy embraced her sister. Really embraced her. But would his darling wife be so sad to see Esther go? That was unclear.

The remainder of Esther's shortened stay had been more pleasant. Dorothy had a renewed confidence, it seemed. And had been more outspoken. Whether that had unnerved Esther or she truly needed to get back East was uncertain. But she was leaving. That *was* certain.

"Have a safe trip." Dorothy fussed over Esther's things, lining them and rearranging them.

"I do hope so. But I don't know that I have any say so in the fact. Although if I did, I think I would—"

"Oh my," Owen cut her off. He pointed in the direction of

the stagecoach as the young man that had driven Esther in came around.

The woman's color drained a bit.

"Should I have a talk with the boy?" Owen offered.

Esther put a hand on his arm. "That is thoughtful of you, Owen. But you need not worry yourself. I can stand on my own two feet. I shall attend to it."

Owen looked at his wife, and they exchanged a smile as Esther moved toward the stagecoach.

"You, there! Sir!"

Pulling his wife a little closer, Owen could not help the chuckle that spilled out into a laugh. That young man was about to get an earful.

August

HEART OF GOLD

Dorothy worked on the gravy pan. There was something about the way that gravy wanted to stick that gave her fits. No matter, she would win.

Amanda grabbed the last of the plates, dried them, and put them back in the dish cabinet. All while humming.

"That's a pretty tune," Dorothy commented. "What's it called?"

"Just some song my mother used to sing. You know, I'm not even sure about the name of it."

Dorothy smiled.

Amanda shut the cabinet and moved back over to Dorothy's side. And just stared.

"Land sakes, child, you're making me jumpy. Whatever is the matter?"

"Well, it seems that this month is...special."

"Special?"

"For you and Uncle Owen."

Dorothy thought for a minute. Oh, yes, their anniversary. Four years married. It felt as if they'd always been married, and yet it also just happened yesterday, didn't it?

They had spent the last couple of anniversaries entertaining others. The Dugans from church took them to dinner last year. And before that, Brandon and Amanda had celebrated them with a special supper. But this year...Dorothy wanted to just be with Owen. They needed some time to themselves. The last couple of weeks, they had been little more than passing each other in the night.

But why was Amanda bringing it up? To let Dorothy know she remembered? Or did she have something up her sleeve?

"Brandon and I really wanted to plan a nice evening for you two. Here. Let me cook, and you just enjoy being among friends. It is your special day, after all."

Dorothy turned back to the water pump, so Amanda wouldn't see her disappointment. "I'll have to check with Owen."

When she turned, she found Amanda's eyes bright and hopeful.

Slowly, Dorothy added, "But I think that will be nice."

Amanda clapped her hands. "It will be wonderful. Just you wait and see. I have some ideas of what to make for you."

Dorothy couldn't deny that something within her sank a little as her sweet friend continued to talk about the possibilities for the evening. Maybe Owen would want it to be just the two of them and would find a way to tell the Millers. Yes, that would be good. And Dorothy wouldn't have to see Amanda's smile turned upside down.

She could hope.

Pulling up to her and Owen's cabin, Dorothy halted the horse and waited. It wasn't long before Owen stepped outside, smiling, and helped her down.

Without anything else, he took the horse's bit and led the animal toward the barn. He was a good man. Helpful and sweet. Surely, he would understand her desire to be alone with him on their anniversary. Yes, he would help her make sure that happened.

She slipped inside and started assembling Owen's supper. And she lost herself in the cooking for several moments. My goodness, how she loved it. Pulling ingredients together and producing something that was worthwhile. And everyone seemed to enjoy it. She loved bringing that added flavor to everyone's day.

There was a time she wondered if she was good at anything. After Esther had married and Dorothy's beau had died, she had looked for purpose beyond herself. Though, she never imagined she'd wind up so far away from home. But a posting for a cook had intrigued her. She'd mustered up the bravery to come all this way to accept the job. And never... okay, rarely...looked back.

The door opened, and Owen stepped within. "Smells great."

He never did tire of her food or leave out the compliments. It did seem he was truly grateful for her abilities in the kitchen. And for her. That suited just fine, because she was so thankful for him.

She heard more than watched him make his way to the kitchen. Was he crazy? He was not going to try and help her, was he? It was difficult not to giggle at the memories of him trying to make her a cake. No, she wouldn't abide him burning their dinner.

"What is it?" She looked over her shoulder as he approached.

"Can't a man want to welcome his wife home?"

She turned. "He can." Careful to keep her messy hands

from touching him, she set her arms around his shoulders and enjoyed his embrace.

After pecking her lips, he pulled her close again.

As much as she loved the warmth and tenderness, she needed to get back to her preparations or they'd never eat. So, she pulled free.

He didn't seem to mind. Just winked before stepping to a dining chair and settling into the sturdy frame. "I got an invite from Eugene today. He wants to treat us to dinner at the café next Thursday."

Dorothy let out a breath but kept her face turned away. How could he not realize that she wanted it to be just the two of them? Did he not want that, too? "Oh?"

"Yeah. I told him that sounded fine."

She grimaced. He couldn't see her features with her back to him. "Well, we might have a problem."

"Problem?"

"Yes. Brandon and Amanda want to have a dinner for us."

"Hmmm. What did you say?"

"I let on that it would be fine."

"Well, that's a pickle."

Dorothy nodded but didn't dare face him. Her heart had sank, and it was bound to be written all over her face. Why didn't he know? Why didn't he understand?

She shoved the chicken pieces into the oven and straightened both her body and demeanor before turning. "Guess we'll have to disappoint someone." Her mind screamed that it shouldn't be her. But she dared not speak that.

"Maybe. I could ask Eugene if we could meet him another day or ask Amanda if we can invite him to the ranch."

"Well, that would work out just fine then, wouldn't it?" A bit of emotion crept into her words, and they came out harsher than she'd intended. She spun back to the stove, wanting to hide her feelings from him.

"Yeah. I suppose it would." The lilt in his voice betrayed his concern.

But if he didn't want to spend the day with just her, she didn't mind these plans, either. That would just be that.

She busied herself preparing vegetables, and everything was silent in the cabin for the next several minutes. Perhaps, she shouldn't be so stubborn, but it was their day. And he had not considered what *she* wanted. It was frustrating.

After pulling their dinner out of the oven, she apportioned his to a plate with some green beans and took it to the table. Setting it in front of him, she all but grunted. "Eat up."

He gave her a curious look, but she was beyond caring. Her heart felt bruised. And her husband didn't understand why.

Dorothy threw back the covers on the bed. Her attitude toward the situation had only gotten worse. Why wouldn't she, then, just tell him? What kept her from expressing herself?

When she glanced at her husband, she noted that he watched her every move.

She didn't care. It wasn't like she hadn't given him a chance. With a *hmph*, she lay down and turned away from him. Though she was angry, she also found herself fighting tears.

No. She would not cry.

"You all right?" A hand settled on her shoulder.

Why did he have to be so gentle and caring? Especially when she was trying to put extra force in her anger to fend off more sensitive emotions welling within.

"I'm fine." The words were all she offered. But they, too, were in a huff.

There was silence. Had he heard her? Decided to let her

be? That made the stirring in her chest ache. Oh well. She would welcome sleep. Not only was she tired, she had become weary of this.

"Dorothy." The word was almost whispered it was so tender.

She bit at her lip as it started to tremble.

"Dorothy, what has you so upset?"

Still, she couldn't—or wouldn't—respond.

"I can't do anything if I don't know what I did."

A tear escaped. How could she let him think such? Sure, his lack of interest in celebrating alone with her had injured her. But he hadn't done it on purpose. He couldn't know how much she wanted that time with just him.

Forcing herself to push words out, she started, "I...just... had hoped..." Emotion overwhelmed her, and she couldn't make herself continue.

"You hoped?" He tugged at her shoulder, urging her to face him. "Hoped what, darling?"

At length, she did shift to her back but kept her regard toward the wall.

"What is it? Will you tell me?" His words, again so soft, so caring.

"It's our anniversary," she blurted out, then squeezed her eyes shut.

"What about it? You don't want to include Eugene?"

She shook her head. "That's not it. Eugene is a good friend."

There was silence from his end as he rubbed her upper arm. Was he considering the situation?

"It's nothing." She sighed. This wasn't a big deal. It would be all right.

"Dorothy?" The word was more a statement than a question.

What more was there to say? She wiped at her eyes and

turned to face him, putting on the bravest face she could muster.

"Would you go on a picnic with me?" His voice was calm and steady. "Just me?"

She widened her eyes. "You mean we'd deny our friends and be just us?"

He nodded. "That's what I really want."

She sat and threw her arms around him. "Me, too. I just...didn't know how to say 'no' to Amanda. And then I thought that you wanted..." The tremble returned to her words.

He stroked her hair. "No. I thought it was what *you* wanted."

She let out a little laugh despite the ache within. "You mean...you were just trying to make me happy?"

"Of course. That's what matters most to me."

She snuggled even closer. "So, we were giving in to each other. Without realizing we wanted the same thing?"

His chest rumbled with light laughter. "Guess so."

"Well, I'll be."

"We're so busy trying to please each other, we neglected the thing that we want most—to celebrate our love." He pressed a kiss to the top of her head.

She settled into him and closed her eyes. This man was so good to her. So good *for* her. And she didn't need the day to look any certain way. The only thing that mattered was that they were together.

For now and always.

As she settled herself on the picnic blanket, Dorothy marveled at the scenery and the man in front of her. He sat on a small stool. There was no way he could get himself off the ground with his bad hip. She rested in the moment, trying to capture everything about it in her heart.

Owen smiled at her. "What are you doing?"

"Just taking it in."

"I'm glad we did this."

"What did Eugene and the Millers say when you told them we were planning to spend the day by ourselves?" She wanted to settle in her mind that all was well.

"What do you mean? Didn't you tell them?" His smile fell.

"No. I thought you were gonna do that." Her breath caught.

Owen stared. And as he did, a smile broke across his face.

"Owen Miller, this isn't funny."

He started to laugh, and it became a big belly laugh before long. "That, my dear, is a matter of opinion."

His laughter was infectious. She found herself giggling at the absurdity of the situation. They had stood their friends up.

But they would face that tomorrow. Because today was for them.

September

AS GOOD AS GOLD

Owen Miller woke early. But not early enough. Dorothy was always up first...well before dawn. He had told her time and again that she needn't worry with him and his breakfast before leaving for Miller Ranch to tend to the family and ranch hands there. But she did. Every. Day.

He had also expressed well enough his desire that she wake him when she rose. The least he could do was help her with her morning preparations. This request, too, it seemed, fell on deaf ears.

Day after day, month after month, the time stretched into their first years of marriage. And nothing changed. Until today.

Owen's eyes opened to the dimness of the cabin as usual. And though he guessed the hour to be the same as when he typically awoke, he knew something was not right.

He sensed the warmth of his wife beside him still. Was she not up and about the kitchen yet? He shifted in the bed. The lack of space and the stiffness in his old bones did not make that easy. In the end, he relented and decided it might be easier if he just rose to a sitting position. And so, he did.

From that angle, it was much easier to look across the mattress at his wife. Just as he had guessed, she still slumbered. Was it earlier than he thought? Had something awoken him in the night?

He glanced at the window and the gentle wisp of the curtains there. Dorothy had asked if they might leave the window open last night and let the breeze cool them as they slept.

The colorful shade of the sky told that dawn approached. His brows furrowed. Perhaps, it was even later than he suspected. Then why was Dorothy still abed?

His eyes fell on her form. Though she often complained these days of being heated, she clutched the blanket close. Surely, she wasn't cold, though. Hadn't he felt heat coming off her?

Reaching a hand to her shoulder, he thought to stir her. That would be best. She would not forgive him if he continued to let her oversleep. But he stopped when his fingers were but inches away. Not only was she warm, she radiated fire, it seemed. Could she be...ill?

Uneasiness poured into his being. Dorothy? Unwell? He had never known her to be so. Though there was no denying it now.

He drew his hand back. What was he to do? Should he go to Miller Ranch and tend to those folks there? Or see to his wife's needs?

Rising, he felt certain he must go and moved for the door. Then changed his mind and turned back to the bed. Only to shift back to the door—his first impulse was best. No, he needed to stay with his wife. But the Millers would be expecting her.

A coughing fit rumbled from Dorothy's form. "You're gonna wear a hole in the floor."

No longer caught with indecision, he stepped around the bed and sought her face.

Her eyes were still closed. But she grimaced. Was she in pain? "Dorothy?"

"Am I?" Her voice was raspy. "I don't feel like myself."

He frowned. "You don't sound like it either."

"Well, aren't you a charmer?"

Touching fingers to her face, he deepened the droop of his mouth. "You need a doctor."

"And you need to mind..." She was caught up in another coughing fit for a moment. "...your manners."

Though she spoke with conviction edged with humor, he wasn't falling for it. The lightness of the moment was slipping away, and there was no longer reason for jest.

"I mean it. You need the doctor."

She waved his hand away. "I just need some more sleep."

He stood straight once more. Perhaps, she was right. Maybe, she did just need a day or two of rest. Glancing at the door, he wondered again—dare he leave her and venture to Miller Ranch? Risk leaving her alone? Or stay with her and let them worry?

"Now, go on with ya." She opened her eyes, and her gaze sought his.

Of course, she wouldn't want to imposition anyone. He swallowed his trepidation.

"Don't let them folks worry themselves into a tizzy. I'll be fine."

Still, he did not move.

Her eyes widened, and she tried to prop up on her elbow. A gray streaked braid fell toward the bed. It was only ever down at night. "You'd best go, or I'll hitch that horse myself."

She sure could talk something fierce. He had to fight the

smile that threatened to break his expression. But he was concerned. Quite concerned.

And she was right. He did need to make his way to Miller Ranch. Only not as her stand in...as if he could be anything close...but to make arrangements for her absence. Yes, he could be just as stubborn.

Owen eased the door to the small cabin open. Was he afraid of his wife?

On his honor, he was.

He'd had a time trying to tear himself away from the ranch without bringing along extra help. But they had agreed to stay put when he pointed out how bad it would be for the younger Millers, should any of them show up sick. Heaven forbid they pass it on to Oliver. So, they relented.

That had been the easy part. Now he would face Dorothy. She did not take kindly to him disregarding her wishes. Though he didn't take too kindly her instructions that he leave her to fend for herself in such a state. Utter nonsense. Stubborn woman.

"Owen?" Her voice croaked from the back of the small structure.

Dare he answer?

Such a pointless exercise.

All the same, he stilled. Why? Hoping she would dismiss the noise she'd heard? He'd have to make his presence known sooner or later. Was he daft?

"Owen?" Her words were stronger. And was that a threatening tone she pressed out under his name? My, she could voice layers into one word like no one else.

"Yes?" His voice quite nearly squeaked. What the devil? Was that his best attempt at innocence? He put his head in a hand and shook it. Then his whole body shook. Laughter. Was he laughing at himself? Or the situation?

"Owen Miller, if that's you, I've got a piece for you."

He jerked his head up. Gone was any hint of humor; it had drained from the moment. He'd best pay the fiddler and face the music. One thing was certain—he couldn't hide forever.

"Coming, sweetheart," he called, as if she hadn't said anything.

He hobbled, perhaps taking his steps even slower than necessary, through the great room. The grumbles from the bedroom were quite audible. And they continued until he stepped to the doorway.

Peering in, he saw that Dorothy had sat up and was leaning against the thin wood of the headboard and the wall. She did *not* look happy.

"There's my sunshine." He smiled. Maybe a bit too big.

She crossed her arms.

Uh oh. The storm clouds were rolling in on him.

"Why are you back so soon?"

He licked his lips, which had become dry all of a sudden. "I—ah—what was that again?"

She raised an eyebrow. The look she shot him could have killed a lesser man. "Why are you back?"

"Oh, that." He attempted to dismiss it as he came around the bed to her side. But he sensed her gaze boring into him every step of the way. "I...ah...wasn't needed."

Her eyes narrowed.

He pulled his regard from her face to the quilt and worked at arranging it. Somehow. He didn't know how, so he made a great show of moving the creases around.

She watched him for a few moments, and then she moved. Her hands struck out like a snake. He couldn't hardly pull his hands back fast enough as she shooed him away.

"You old goat, I told you I expected you to do my part.

That was our deal. I would stay only if you would do the cooking today."

Was it hot in here? And how was it possible for his mouth to stay so dry? "See, there wasn't much cause for me, with Amanda there."

"Posh! She has that baby to look after. And she's terrible tired as it is."

Owen looked toward the window. Why hadn't he planned this part out? After several seconds of silence, he shrugged and threw his hands up. "All right, Dorothy. You got me. You've found me out." He hobbled back to the door. "I didn't intend to stay there for one minute longer than it took to tell Brandon and Amanda what was going on. There! You happy?"

She pushed out a "*hurumph.*"

"Yes, I know...my sin is great. Unpardonable even. But I did it for *you.*"

Her gaze fell on him again. There was the parched mouth, dry as cotton. With it came the sweats though. Too much moisture on his face and none in his mouth. What a combination.

Still, he squared his shoulders and glared back. "Now, I'm gonna go into that kitchen and..."

"*My* kitchen?"

He closed his eyes briefly before continuing. "...I'm going into that kitchen, *our* kitchen, and make you something that will fill your belly and give you some nourishment. And I don't want to hear another word about it."

When he turned to leave, he ground his teeth. No matter how determined he had been when putting those words forth, his voice had still squeaked. He was helpless indeed when it came to that woman. Completely helpless.

"What do you think, doctor?" Owen tried to look around the man. He was about to go out of his boots with worry after Dorothy.

The man was perhaps too young to be doctoring people, much less someone so important.

Bright eyes turned and looked at Owen. "You've got to stop leaning over me, Mr. Miller. I can't do a proper exam with you at my shoulder."

Owen frowned and backed away. So, he offended the young doctor...well the child, barely a man. He smirked behind the doctor's back. Made him feel a little better.

"I'd rather you not be in here at all, to tell you the truth of it." The doctor rummaged in his black case for something. At last, he pulled out a strange looking tool and held it up to Dorothy's ear.

Owen was not deterred. He would rather have a doctor who wasn't wet behind the ears. People couldn't always get their 'rathers.' But he held his tongue. It wouldn't do anyone any good for him to voice those thoughts.

The next several minutes passed in hours, it seemed. But, at length, the doctor put all the strange objects back into his bag and leaned away from Dorothy. He patted her arm. "You'll be just fine. It's a seasonal sickness. Not much I can do except give you medicines to make you comfortable. But rest and broth are the best things for you."

How did she not roll her eyes at that?

She would have, if Owen had said it.

Instead, she rearranged that confounded quilt while offering the doctor a tight smile. "I thank you. Perhaps, I should get to resting now."

The doctor nodded, grabbed the bag's handle, and rose.

"Let me see you out," Owen offered. He worked to contain the laughter bubbling up. The man-child seemed rather oblivious to Dorothy's dismissal and her platitudes.

Escorting the man out and thanking him for his services took little effort. But as Owen closed the door, he was faced with the reality that Dorothy had been upset. She was a woman who liked action and enjoyed being busy. How would she manage days abed, resting? How would he make it any more pleasant for her? That would be quite a task, indeed.

He garnered his courage and moved back to the bedroom.

Dorothy had turned toward the wall, her back to him. By all appearances, she slept. Only...

He knew better. She was unsettled. And she could never sleep when she was so undone. The only question was whether or not she would welcome his company. But he had to try. So, he walked to her side of the bed and stood, waiting for her to notice him.

When she did spot him soon after he came around the foot of the bed, she sealed her eyes. "I don't have it in me, Owen." Her voice wavered as her sentence ended.

He moved closer and put a hand over hers. "It's not forever, darling. You know you'll be up before he thinks you will."

She sniffled.

"You have always beat the odds."

Everything stilled in that moment. She opened her mouth. And he thought she prepared to counter his statement. But she didn't.

Her mouth set once more, and she swallowed.

"'Sides, you've got me. If nothing else, you gotta get better before I *really* mess up your kitchen."

Her gaze flew to him. "You jest."

He leaned back, folding his arms in front of himself and smiled. "Maybe. Maybe not."

And then he saw it. Slight. Maybe only just there. But it was there, he felt certain of it—the faintest hint of a smile.

But it meant the world to him.

Owen stretched. His body protested every movement. He couldn't remember the last time he ached so. The evening had not been kind to him. But he would do it again. For her.

He rose from his armchair. How did he even sleep in that thing? That was not clear. But he must have been tired enough after the previous day for sleep to capture him. Though the night's rest had been fitful—what else could he expect?

Now on his feet, unsteady at that, he shuffled one foot forward.

That was a mistake.

He grabbed for the back of the chair to keep upright.

Confounded hip! Would he ever be capable of the simple things in life? Or would he forever be infirm? A burden on those he cared about.

He sighed, trying to push all the frustration from his body, feeble as it was. Nothing would be gained by wallowing in pity. That would render him less than useless. High time he gathered what strength he could muster and check on Dorothy.

Hobbling did not quite describe the manner in which he maneuvered himself to the bedroom. He nearly cleared every shelf and counter on the way in his clumsy attempts to keep his momentum.

It took only moments, however, before he neared the bedroom door. The sound of Dorothy's coughing greeted him.

He frowned. That was not a good sign.

Pushing the door, already open just a bit, he made the gap wide enough for him to pass through. And to take full stock of the situation.

Dorothy sat on the edge of the bed, legs over the side. Her

gray streaked brown hair tumbled down her back, much of it loosened from her braid.

Why was she on the side of the bed? Did she intend to get up? Had she need of something?

"Can I help?" His voice croaked more than he'd like. The last thing he needed was for her to be concerned after him.

"Help me?" she asked as she turned. An eyebrow shot up. Her throat pulsed. Did she work to suppress more coughing? The hair around her face was damp. Had she been overheated through the night? Was she still afire with fever?

"Let's get you back into bed." He drew closer.

"No need." She held up a hand in his direction as if to ward him off.

"Pardon?" What could she mean? Her features were more drawn than one of those political cartoons everyone in town was so fond of.

"I..." She paused and licked her lips, giving her regard to the bedclothes. Was she uncertain of herself? "I seemed to have quite recovered." Her gaze found his.

Though her words may have sounded confident, she could not hide her trepidation from him. Not in those eyes he knew so well.

"That so?" He leaned away from her. And immediately regretted it when his back about gave out.

She firmed her jaw and raised her chin. "Sure is. Why, I...I think I'll get ready and head out to the ranch."

"Oh? You're that well, are ya?"

Her eyes narrowed. Why was the intensity of her glare so painful?

He wanted to step away but held his ground. "Ready for cookin' and cleanin'?"

She nodded. "I ain't never let a little thing like this keep me down for long." Rising, though a bit unsteady at first, she then crossed her arms. As if daring him to challenge her.

He only nodded.

"So, I'll thank you to wipe that smirk off your face and leave me to my ablutions."

"Your what?"

She rolled her eyes. "My morning things. The getting ready things." Turning from him, she moved to the water pitcher and wash bowl.

He nodded again and moved to leave, more strength in his step. But he halted at the door. "Just one thing...you're sure enough that you won't be risking them folk and those little ones?"

She paused her movements. He noted how heavily she leaned on the washbowl's stand.

He wasn't ready to let her off, though. "I say, I'd feel mighty guilty if I got that sweet Louise sick. Or worse— Oliver. My, my, my...I sure am glad you're all better, so you don't have to worry about that."

Shifting back in the direction of the door, he hid his smile.

"Oliver? You think I have—um, *had*—something that's catchin'?"

His smile broadened. But he forced his features to return to their more serious lines before he turned to face her. "Most certainly. But there's no cause for worry. Seein' as your better now."

She didn't move, remaining paused as she had been with her hands inches above the bowl and dripping with water. He had gotten to her. Was it the victory he'd wanted though? Or had he hurt her?

Two uneven strides carried him to her side. Picking up the cloth, he then wrapped it around her hands and made gentle strokes over her skin. Only then did he notice the slight tremble in her. From the water? The illness? Or something he'd said?

"Do you...think it would be better if I...?" Her sentence trailed off. Was she so uncertain?

"I think you are well enough entitled, sweetheart, to take another day of rest." His task complete, he put the now damp cloth down and took her hands in his, giving them a gentle squeeze. "And I'll take care of you. If you'll let me."

Her eyes focused and shifted to meet his gaze. Though her lips remained a thin line, her eyes glistened and danced just enough to give him every hope that she saw him and his heart for her.

He lifted one hand to touch the side of her face. "First things first—let's get you back in bed."

She let out a deep breath. Her body slackened, as if the exhale had depleted her. And she let him lead her to her rest.

And he had hope that for once in their marriage, she might let him share the burdens she bore.

Owen settled into his armchair. Dorothy was beside him in her own. Today had been busy and tiring. But a good busy. He was worn with having worked and served his wife well.

And he wouldn't have it any other way.

"Take a load off them bones." She grinned.

He returned the smile. "Will do."

She patted his hand.

He flipped his over and captured her fingers.

"Oh, you old charmer." Her cheeks reddened.

And he once again enjoyed the thought that he could still make his bride blush. He took it one step further and lifted her hand to his lips for a gentle kiss.

She swatted at him with her other hand but did not pull the one he held away. "You just beat all."

He laughed.

They had been able to spend much time together these last several days. And it had been precious. Even more so when she started feeling more herself.

Owen had worried she might insist on returning to her work at the ranch straight away, but she hadn't. She heeded his words about taking things slowly. Or was it that she had been enjoying their time as much as he?

Would he ever tire of this woman?

"What's in your head?" She freed her hand to give his arm a poke.

"Huh?" He startled.

"You're awful quiet," she said. Her eyes gleamed. "I don't like it."

He chuckled. "No. Not up to anything."

She gave him a sideways glance. "And I'm supposed to believe that?" The smirk on her features told that she did already.

"I was just thinkin'."

"Oh my, it's worse!" She put a hand to her chest.

"Much worse."

"Well, you'd best spit it out. I can handle it." She continued to clutch at the fabric over her heart.

His mouth broadened. "Just thinking about how much I've enjoyed this past week."

Her lips tilted into a sweet smile. And her eyes seemed to shine in the lantern light.

He continued. "I know you didn't have it easy, being sick and all—"

"Now you hush that, right now." Her tone bit. "I'll hear none of it. Not a bit."

He watched her as the light flickered on her face.

"I am so full of blessing, I'm about to burst."

Owen's brow lifted. Could she mean that?

"No one has ever taken such care of me. Ever."

He glanced down at their joined hands. What could he say?

But her voice broke into the moment. "And I'm afraid that's part my own fault."

Lifting his face, he watched for the emotions that would play on her features. But she seemed resolute.

"But you...you wouldn't leave well enough alone. Determined." She let out a laugh. "No—stubborn. Yeah...that's you, for sure."

One side of his mouth rose, surely it made for a lop-sided grin.

"And I can't thank you enough."

What?

"You stepped in when I needed you. And even faced me down when it was necessary."

The way her eyes glistened, he was certain there would be tears. But she turned away and wiped at her eyes before one could betray her.

"I didn't think you would let me. You've always been the one to take on everyone else's problems. See to everyone else's needs. Especially mine."

She turned back to him. And watched, waiting. Now that was definitely not like her.

But he continued. "I've been a burden on you. For too long, I—"

"Now, you stop that. You are no burden! You are my husband. My friend. My partner."

A thickness welled in his chest, rising in him, nearly choking out his words. So, he brought her hand to his lips again until he could speak. Then he met her gaze. "And this week, I felt like it."

Something pulled Owen from the sweet respite of sleep. Not just any sleep. But restful sleep...in his own bed. Beside his loving wife. When he came to himself enough to realize someone shook him, his first thought was that something had happened to Dorothy. His eyes shot open, and he jerked up as much as he could.

"Dorothy..." His voice was ragged and groggy.

"Yes, it's me." Her figure loomed over him. "Well, don't act so surprised to find me in your bed...excuse me...*our* bed."

He ran a hand down his face to attempt to remove the cobwebs of lingering sleep from his mind. It did not help much. "Are you ill?"

"No. I am getting up to do my ablutions."

"Your wh—? Never mind."

"And I thought you might could start some breakfast for us."

Working his brain as quickly as possible through the haze, he considered her words. And he realized.

"Yes, ma'am." He smiled and slid his legs off the side of the bed.

Gone was the Dorothy who treated him as if he were someone to be catered to. And now emerged a true partnership.

For as long as they both should live.

October

SOLID GOLD

Owen Miller walked through the barn. Just a once over. A check. Dorothy would be home soon, and then they would get started on their preparations for the Harvest Day Festival.

Everything here seemed to be in order. Not a speck out of place—

A shuffling sound off to the right and behind him gave him pause. He jerked around to confront whatever danger lay there. Sharp pain radiated from his hip, and he crumpled onto his side.

Breathing heavily and attempting to steady himself against the intense throbbing, he looked to where the sound had come from. A squirrel raced out of the barn.

That varmint! Had probably come looking for a free meal. Now here Owen lay, in a heap. Could he get up? Could he even move?

Pushing up on his hands, which stung from the impact with the ground, he managed to get into a sitting position. But the pain that shot through him every few seconds, in addition to the constant dull ache, all but stole his breath. How was it that a fifteen-year-old injury still plagued him so? He wasn't one to pity himself...still there were times when he wished he could go back. But what would he do different? Not be thrown from that horse? Perhaps, not try to ride the unrideable stallion. That pride of his...

The pain brought him back to the present, and he looked at the barn opening. How could he do this? It would not be good for Dorothy to find him like this. Have to help him up and to the house.

He had to try...

Determination filled him. He would get up somehow and into the house, if it was the last thing he did. Maneuvering to the side, he pushed again while dragging his leg. Pressing and shifting, he worked to gain his feet. But it wasn't happening. He collapsed once more.

That still didn't mean he had to give up. He glanced about the area. The post outside the stable had a couple of hooks that he might use as handholds. Would that be all he needed?

He worked his way onto his belly; pain gripped him every time he inched his hip forward. And, little by little, he progressed. Several minutes later, and three times as long as he'd expected, he could touch the post. But he didn't press on. He needed a moment to gather himself. Sweat trickled down his face, and every part of him felt heated. Still, he refused to lie there and wait for help. He could do this. He would.

Grabbing at the bench beside the stall door, he leveraged it against his weight. It was no easy task. Soon enough, he had upward momentum. Clinging to the hooks on the post, he slinked upright.

But even when standing, he leaned on his good leg, somewhat nervous to set his foot on the ground. Much less put weight on it. How would he get to the cabin, up the front porch stairs, and inside without doing so? He couldn't hop on the good leg. That wouldn't work.

Exasperated and spent, he sunk onto the bench. Maybe it wouldn't be the worst thing for Dorothy to find him here. At least, he wasn't face down in the dirt. Perhaps, his pride could survive.

Not a chance.

Regardless, he was stuck. It could have been hours before he heard the horse closing in on the property, he wasn't certain. He might have lost consciousness as he leaned against the stable. He just wasn't sure. One glance at how light it was outside told him that it couldn't have been near that long.

The horse and cart came to a stop just outside, between the barn and the cabin. Should he call for her? Or let her discover him? It was probably better he have somewhat of a handle on this.

"Dorothy?" he yelled out. Surprised at the weakness of his voice.

No sound.

"Dorothy?"

"Owen?" came her reply. "Where are you? The barn?"

"Yes. I...fell."

"Gracious! Are you hurt?"

He heard the slight squeal of the wagon as she dismounted. Then the rustle of her skirt and gentle thud of her boots on the firm ground. She was coming.

"I'm in one piece." He slid his eyes closed and wondered at her expression upon finding him. But he could not make himself look.

"Owen!" Her raised tone betrayed that she had spotted him.

Her footfalls drew closer. Only then did he lift his eyelids. By that time, she was only a foot or two away. When she reached him, she crouched down, her gaze taking him in. Her features contorted—concern and worry filled them.

"Honest. I'm all right. I just...don't know that I can walk by myself."

She shook her head as her gaze traveled up toward his face. "You're not all right. You're bleeding."

What? Bleeding?

Delicate fingers reached for his cheek.

That must have been why the side of his face had stung as the sweat moved across it. "It's not bad."

She gave him a disbelieving look. "How would you know?" Tenderly, her fingertips touched the scrapes that only she could see.

"Quit worrying, woman. I'll live." He tried to smile.

It was not well received.

"Let's get you inside." She moved to his right side, putting hands on his waist as he set an arm around her shoulders.

And together, they got him to his feet. He moved forward, leaning on her more than he wanted to. That was short lived. As he gingerly set the tiniest bit of weight on the bad leg, it gave way. If she hadn't been there, he would have fallen again.

He seethed through his teeth.

She frowned. "We'll go slow."

It was quite a while later before Dorothy was easing him into his armchair. Her breaths came in heaves, same as his. That had been a bit of work for both of them. But he was sad to note that he was rather worn out. He didn't know if he could stay alert much longer.

Dorothy bit at her lip. Something was bothering her.

"What is it?" He struggled to keep the irritability with himself out of his voice.

"I want to go for the doctor, but I can't make myself leave you like this."

"I tell you, I'll be fine. Just resting."

She grimaced. Not only did she not believe him, she wasn't going to leave. He didn't think this merited the doctor's attention necessarily. What could he say that he hadn't already?

Owen heard another horse and cart outside. Who would be dropping in on them?

"Oh, that's Mariena." Dorothy moved to the window and looked outside. "Sure enough."

"Mariena?" Why was she coming by?

"Amanda is sending her for some cinnamon. We were getting things together to start baking for the Harvest Day festivities. But the General Store was out."

Owen straightened himself in the chair, nearly crying out at the stabbing in his hip.

"No, you don't," Dorothy said. "Stay put."

Knock, knock.

Dorothy opened the door.

Owen couldn't see, but he heard Mariena's voice. "Good afternoon, Cook."

"Am I ever glad to see you!" Dorothy reached outside and pulled the woman in.

Mariena's eyes were wide as she scanned the area. Once they settled on Owen, she frowned. "What is the matter?"

"It's Owen. He fell. I need the doctor...*he* needs the doctor. But I can't leave him."

"I will send Cutie."

Cutie was there? Owen was certain he'd die of embarrassment.

Mariena disappeared, and Dorothy watched out the door until she returned.

"He will be back with the doctor as quickly as he can."

"Now this is entirely too much fussin'. It isn't so bad."

Dorothy shot him a look that paused his movements. "You will be seen."

He nodded and avoided Mariena's gaze.

"Are you comfortable?" Dorothy closed the distance to him in a hurry. "Maybe we," she said, indicating Mariena and herself, "can get you to the bed."

"Leave well enough alone. I'm just fine right here."

Dorothy didn't look happy with his insistence. But he was doing everything he could to maintain some of his dignity.

"Let me put on some coffee," Mariena said, moving into the kitchen.

"I don't know what's got into you, Owen Miller. But you need all the help we can get right now."

He leaned back against the chair and let his eyes close once more. She was right. And he couldn't deny it.

Long after the doctor had left, with no new advice given other than orders to rest, Mariena and Cutie lingered. They had left their little one with Amanda and her brood. It all seemed rather providential. Except that Owen hated the whole thing: the fall, the pain, the help, the doting...all of it.

He was now in the bedroom and could only hear snatches of the conversation. Not enough to make out anything. But he guessed Cutie and Mariena had left when he heard the front door close.

Moments later, Dorothy slipped into the room. "How are you?"

"For the hundredth time, I'm well enough. No need for all this fuss."

She didn't speak for a while, just came to his side of the bed and sat on the mattress. "You worried me today, you old goat."

"I know," he said on a sigh.

"And I'm not sure what to do now."

"What do you mean?" He shifted, grimacing anew at the pain.

"You need tending. And I have a list of things to get done for the Harvest Day Festival." She met his gaze. "But that's not your problem."

"It sort of is."

She looked away.

"Can you hand off some of your responsibilities?" It seemed fair enough, didn't it?

She shrugged. "Mariena offered to come tomorrow and help me get things done."

"That's...wonderful." Owen wasn't sure his wife saw it that way. She had a stubborn streak in her, too.

"Oh, I don't know."

Owen thought for a minute and found inspiration in the words she had spoken to him earlier that day. "I don't know what's got into you, Dorothy Miller. But you need all the help we can get right now."

Her eyes became wider. Did she realize that he had thrown her words back at her? He would wager so. And for a moment, he could've sworn that she was about to have a fit.

But instead, a slow smile filled her face. "Sounds about right. Words of wisdom."

He reached for her hand and gripped it. "I'm thankful for you."

She set her other hand on their clasped two. "You know I am, too."

"We'll get through this. Together."

She nodded. "Together."

Owen settled into the seat Dorothy selected for them in the church yard. Everything was so nice. Things had really come together for the festival. They always did. Over the last couple of days, Mariena had been a faithful help to Dorothy. For which he was grateful. It enabled his wife to tend to him in the way he needed. Whether he wanted it or not.

But now, he was glad his hip was much improved. He could come out and enjoy the Harvest Day Festival because his good behavior had led to some added strength.

As much as the last days had tried his pride, he had been thankful. For it brought him and Dorothy closer in a special way. He had indeed needed her assistance. And she had been a willing and capable help.

She took the seat next to him and moved closer. "You good?"

"I am."

"Did I set you up okay? You're not in pain?"

"I told you I'm good, woman. Now quit your yappin' and let me enjoy the day."

They watched the families young and old scurrying here and there. Indeed, even Mariena busied herself setting up her and Dorothy's dishes.

"Thank you for pushing me to accept Mariena's help. I couldn't have done everything without her."

He grasped her hand and squeezed it. "I know exactly what you mean."

"Guess we both needed a healthy dose of humility this week."

He nodded and wrapped an arm around his wife. "I like having you to myself, though."

She smiled. "I promised I would stay by your side. In sickness and in health. Easiest promise in the world to make. A little harder when it plays out."

He looked into her eyes. And he knew it wasn't that she

regretted the decision. But she acknowledged the difficulty of the last few days. It must be hard—seeing your loved one in pain and in such need. She had soldiered through. His amazing Dorothy.

Leaning in her direction, he pressed a kiss into her hair. "I think the best is yet to come."

When she turned to look at him, there was a hint of her concern remaining. Did she think it would be downhill for him? That the best was behind them? He wouldn't let this keep him down. But he would also not let his pride keep him from asking for help.

"I know it," he said low.

She wiped at the side of her face. Had a tear escaped? Was she so emotional?

"I promise." His lips tugged upward.

Hers responded in kind.

No matter what the future held, he knew they could face it. Together.

November

SILENCE IS GOLDEN

The day had been pleasant, and things were settling for the evening as Dorothy washed her and Owen's dinner dishes. The week had barely started, and there was much ado in town about the election yesterday. Owen grabbed for the paper, readying himself to read, once she finished her cleaning.

He had brought the paper from town earlier today but promised he had not so much as peeked at it yet. They had agreed they would absorb the news together.

She was both excited and nervous about the outcome. What would it mean? What would any changes in Congress bring? Dorothy had never been overly political. In fact, she preferred not to discuss such things. However, that did not mean that she didn't care.

"I'm ready." She sat down and took in a deep breath.

He looked over the paper. Was he trying to decide what was relevant to her? As if she couldn't discern that herself?

She blew out pent up air. There was no need to get in a huff. Owen knew better. And he respected her.

Owen straightened the folds of the local paper and started

to read. His tone deepened and slowed, reflecting his disappointment.

The Republicans had lost the House to the Democrats.

Dorothy gritted her teeth. If only the territories could vote. If only women could vote...

That was a big dream indeed. And becoming more of a fight with each passing day. Many women were dedicated to the effort. And while Dorothy wasn't on the forefront, she watched closely.

This loss yesterday to the Democratic Party would not spell good things for Women's Suffrage. While she didn't trust any politician to seek anyone's good but their own, the Republican Party had, by and large, been more favorably inclined to the movement.

"Does it..." She cleared her throat. "Is there any news about a vote on the women's suffrage?"

Soft eyes fell on hers, but he shook his head.

Nothing. There had been no effort made by Congress apart from appointing that special committee earlier this year. But in June, the report they gave seemed favorable. Too bad it never led to an actual vote. Were the politicians playing a game? Were they nervous for their careers if they actually put their 'yay' or 'nay' on paper?

She closed her eyes and asked God for peace. What would the future hold? Would little Louise Miller ever be able to vote? As a citizen and a woman? Dorothy could hope. And pray.

Owen reached across the table and grabbed her hand. "It will all work out."

"How can you say that? How can you know?"

"Because God is in control. Always has been, always will be. And sniffling politicians cannot thwart His purposes for mankind. Or for the United States of America."

She sighed and tried to find comfort in the truth of his words. But her heart still twisted with doubt.

"Let's think on something more pleasant, shall we? No use getting worn with these things that *we* can't control."

She nodded. "Besides, I've got too much going on to be butting heads with anyone."

He smiled. "That's my girl."

"Amanda told me that Brandon's mother will be here by Thanksgiving."

"It will be good to see her again. Things have been hard on her since Charles passed." There was a catch in his throat.

Dorothy turned her hand over to interlink their fingers. "She's not the only one."

He watched her. Did he wonder after her statement? Did he think she didn't notice how difficult losing his brother had been?

But she knew he would rather not dwell on that. Grief was a strange thing. "She said one of Brandon's cousins—David— will be traveling with her. Is that your sister's boy?"

"No. That's one of Sylvia's kin. Her brother's son, I think."

"It's hard to keep track, I know."

"'Specially as I get older."

Dorothy gave him a cross look. "Now, don't you go starting that. Next thing you know, you'll be calling *me* old."

Owen leaned in, his eyebrows arched, his features taking on a humorous appearance. "I would never dream of it."

Dorothy hummed while she worked. Getting everything tidy before dinner was such a chore. But nothing she couldn't handle. My, how she missed the older ranch hands. Cutie, Dan, and Slim may have given her fits at times, but these younger boys could sure make a mess! She wiped at the wooden table, trying to corral the crumbs left behind. Heaven forbid they make it to her clean floor.

A small cloud of dust appeared on the horizon in the direction of town. Was Brandon back already? He had left earlier to fetch his mother and cousin from the station. It didn't seem possible he could have been there and back already. Unless she had lost track of time.

She hurried through cleaning the table. And was thankful she had finished the rest of the home before now. Stepping back, she surveyed first the great room and dining area and then the kitchen.

Sylvia Miller would step into a freshened homestead. That brought a smile to Dorothy's face and a swelling in her chest. The state of this house would reflect her abilities. And she had done herself proud. Now, if dinner could go off without a hitch...

On the other side of the wall to the porch, a chair creaked. Owen must be getting to his feet. Her husband had both looked forward to and dreaded Sylvia's arrival. He was genuinely glad she came. But her coming without Charles... that made Owen's brother's passing all the more real.

Dorothy warred between staying in her place and going to her husband's side. But not for long. Owen needed her close. So, she stepped out onto the porch to find him clinging to a post near the porch's edge.

She stepped to him. "Shall we go out to greet them? Or would you prefer to wait here?"

Owen's gaze remained trained on the coming wagon.

Dorothy turned that way. She could discern the three figures now. She was tempted to slide her hand into Owen's. But, as much as he would want her by his side, he probably needed that last bit of space to process without her pushing herself on him.

"Let's do that," he finally said, his words coming out measured. Was he attempting to hold back emotion?

It seemed only right that she slide an arm around his elbow. He didn't look at her, but he tensed the arm, giving her something to hold to. She was glad for the physical connection and prayed it would give him support.

They maneuvered to the stairs and then into the yard directly in front of the house. Amanda stood there already, holding little Oliver. And a young Louise clung to her ma's skirt. The child had grown so much in the last few years. Would her grandmother even recognize her? Louise had been a toddler when the family went to Richmond after Charles's death. It was doubtful she would have any memory of the older woman.

There the ragtag bunch stood, waiting on the horse and cart. They weren't waiting long before Brandon slowed the animal on approach and eased the wagon into place. He tipped his hat to his wife and the elder Millers. Then hopped down, coming around the wagon to his mother's side of the cart.

Once he dropped off the bench, Dorothy could see Sylvia better. She looked as if she had aged more years than existed between their last meeting. And she wore all black, though her time of mourning had long passed. Did this indicate that she had not moved on within, as well?

Dorothy pressed a smile to her features when Sylvia waved to them. The woman's face lit up, shedding some of the years in an instant.

Brandon's cousin was a fine-looking man. But he wasn't built like the ranch hands. He was slender and looked every bit the manner of man who didn't get his hands dirty. Would he dread his stay here? Would he judge the homestead as quaint and small? She prayed not, for she was not totally responsible for what her mouth did if he said such.

Soon enough, Brandon escorted his mother to the small waiting entourage.

Amanda moved toward her mother-in-law, Louise trailing and Oliver grasping for a better handhold. The two women embraced, and Dorothy noticed that they exchanged words. Though they weren't so far away, they kept their tones too quiet for Dorothy to overhear.

Over Amanda's shoulder, Sylvia's gaze landed on Owen.

Dorothy felt him stiffen and thought she saw glistening in Sylvia's eyes. Even if it had been years, Dorothy remembered thinking that Owen and his brother were similar in appearance. This would be a difficult exchange.

As Amanda released her, Sylvia patted Oliver's back and put a hand to Louise's shoulder. The small girl tried to hide in the folds of Amanda's skirt. Hopefully, Sylvia wouldn't hold that against her.

Eli appeared as if from thin air. Had the ranch hand been in the barn? He began working to unload the first trunk.

When Dorothy refocused on the people around her, she found that Sylvia drew nearer.

Owen released his wife and opened his arms for his sister-in-law. Dorothy didn't have it in her to question the gesture or judge him. There was too much unresolved grief in his heart. Instead, she prayed that this visit would be healing for him.

When he embraced Sylvia, she saw his shoulders shake, just slightly. Everything in Dorothy wanted to lay a hand on his back, his shoulder, something to reassure him. But that was not needed. He knew she was there, and she had to trust in this process, let him lean into his grief for now.

They parted, and Dorothy saw that Sylvia's tears had started making their way down her face. She pulled out her handkerchief. Why had Owen not offered his? Dorothy looked and found that he used his own in a show of rubbing his nose, but he couldn't hide the moisture from her.

"Well, now," announced the cousin. "Isn't this quaint."

Dorothy turned on the man. How calloused to intrude on this moment. How rude to say such about his cousin's home. She drew in a breath, ready to give him a piece of her mind.

Owen's hand found hers, and he squeezed it while giving her a meaningful look.

She sighed and swallowed her words. Just because David was taking this moment and turning it toward himself didn't mean she had to. But no one could stop her from stabbing at him with her gaze.

Dorothy ferried the last of the breakfast dishes to the dining table. She smiled at her husband as she set the bacon near him. He winked at her, and it warmed her from within. How was that possible? She was no blushing young girl—but even as a mature woman more than four years married, he could still give her tingles.

Thanksgiving would be in a week, and she might as well start on the preparations today. It would be special having Sylvia and David here. But Dorothy felt all the more pressured to get it just right. She might should make a list of her food needs today. Brandon's favorite, hickory nut cake, was a certainty. Now, what kind of bird would they have this year—chicken, goose, turkey?

And then she noticed everyone stared at her. What was going on? She felt the urge to escape into the kitchen. Maybe that was why they gawked. She didn't typically linger in the dining space.

Brandon cleared his throat. "What do you say, Cook?"

Had someone asked her something? She had been so lost in thought she had missed it entirely. Dare she admit to it?

Owen pulled out the chair beside himself. "I've got a place for you right here."

Had they wanted her to join them? That was odd. Not that they didn't always welcome her presence at the meal, but she was most often too busy running here and there that everyone had come to accept that she wasn't going to sit.

"Please," Amanda said, rising. "We would like you to join us and actually eat with us for a change."

Dorothy's heart stuttered at the kindness. But she couldn't sit. She had too much to do. "But I—"

Owen grabbed her hand. "It can wait."

She met his gaze. It was sweet, to be sure. It was also easier for him to think that. How could he understand what all she had to do today? He was such an interference.

Dorothy scanned the faces. What could she say now that wouldn't disrespect Owen? And to be fair, he might be right. Even if only this once.

At length, she jerked her head in a nod. "Let me grab a plate."

"I've got it." Amanda moved into the kitchen before Dorothy could protest.

Owen arched his brows.

She had nothing left to do but sit. So, she did.

Amanda slid a plate in front of her and then rejoined her own husband.

They all clasped hands as Brandon prayed over the meal. And then they went about filling their plates.

What was she to do? She still wasn't certain she could actually eat in front of everyone. Maybe she could just enjoy the conversation.

But when Owen passed the biscuits and she made a move to send them on, he laid a hand on her arm. "Please. Eat."

She studied him. Did he not understand how uneasy this made her?

"For me."

How could she say 'no' to that? He was so earnest and caring, she melted. And grabbed a biscuit for her plate.

Conversation flowed. Dorothy continued to feel awkward being at the table, but she also found herself relaxing into the care and consideration everyone had for each other.

"I meant to ask you, David," Brandon was saying. "How did you end up coming along with Mother?"

The man in question looked up from his plate and blotted his mouth with his napkin. "Were you not aware that George took ill?"

"Yes, I had heard that your brother was unable to come. But I thought Mother decided to make the trip alone."

"She did. And was I ever surprised at that. Can you imagine? A woman...much less a woman of her age...coming to this wild frontier on her own?"

"Oh, come now." Sylvia spoke up. "I'm not so helpless."

David held up a hand. "Aunt Sylvia, you have no idea the kinds of dangers that exist for women. Especially out here."

Brandon appeared stricken. Still, when he opened his mouth, he only said, "I appreciate your readiness to ensure my mother's comfort and safety on the trip. But I don't think—"

"It was rather fortunate that I was able to escort her. I do have such a compassion for others. And I couldn't bear the thought of something happening to my favorite aunt." He smiled sweetly at Sylvia.

The whole exchange ruffled Dorothy's feathers. To think that a woman was incapable. And to further insult her because of her age...it pushed the boundaries of Dorothy's ability to stay silent.

"Women these days are just blind to the trouble out there. They need someone reliable to care for them."

Brandon opened his mouth, but it was Owen whose voice fell over the room. "The next thing you know, they'll be expecting to vote." The slight tilt to the corners of his lips let Dorothy know he only poked David and jested with her and the others.

David nearly interrupted him in his hurry to add. "Can you imagine? Women...voting? What a disaster that would be! The female mind cannot possibly work out the intricacies of the political scene. Not enough to make an informed decision."

"That's not quite what I meant," Owen interjected into the exchange.

"Oh, I assure you, I understand very well what you are saying." David pushed his plate away from himself. "These... ladies...pushing for the vote lack the ability to comprehend the magnitude of their actions. It won't happen. Not in this lifetime. Not ever."

There was silence around the table. Color had risen to Brandon's face. He clearly wasn't happy with his cousin. Amanda had stopped eating and just stared at the man across the table.

"Now, David." Sylvia spoke up. "Don't be so harsh. They mean well. And I think you underestimate the women of your acquaintance."

He looked at his aunt as if she were a child who had asked a ridiculous question. "I'm certain you must think so."

Dorothy coughed, her bite not quite finding its way into the correct path to her stomach.

Owen turned to her, concern in his eyes.

She put a hand on his, patting it, trying to assure him she was well. After wiping her mouth, she drew in a breath. Someone had to set this man straight. Whether or not she cared to discuss politics, she would not...could not sit here and listen to this man insult every woman in earshot and condescend her sister-in-law.

Owen's hand squeezed hers.

She was grateful for his support. "David, do you really think—"

A quick jerk on her arm gave her pause. Her gaze sought her husband's. Why would he want to prevent her from continuing? The hardness in his eyes seemed to bid her hold her tongue. Why? Whatever for? The man was sorely mistaken in his opinion. And she wanted to give him a piece of her mind.

Owen's intervention both vexed and confused her. But she trusted him. Even if the earful would be directed at him later. So, she held her tongue.

David's brows lifted as he settled his regard on her.

She swallowed the words that fought for release and just said, "Do you think you are finished?" Not the best...but it allowed her to turn the conversation. "Did you enjoy your eggs?"

He scooted his chair back slightly. "I...yes." His face was a mask. Had he truly liked them? "It's not often I get to indulge in such rustic flare."

What did he say? Now, he would speak down about her cooking? Why, she never! The desire to speak rose once more. But a quick look at Owen bade her continue to keep the loosely held peace. She would lay it all out for Owen when she had a chance. While she had no desire to shame her husband, she wouldn't abide him silencing her this way.

Dorothy waited for Owen to gain the wagon bench. She was eager for it to be just the two of them. There was a lot on her mind and she had to get it out. Even if it meant unloading it on him. After all, wasn't he deserving? He hadn't let her unleash her frustration on the person who had earned it.

Owen settled next to her and slapped the reins.

Dorothy gave a gentle wave to Amanda and Brandon, who were on the porch. But she couldn't make herself smile. That was not going to happen with so much pent-up frustration welling within her.

"You're awful quiet," Owen said as they pulled away from the homestead.

She held back from responding. They weren't far enough away. She could bide her time.

They continued to ride with nothing further. Was Owen content with this tension between them? That didn't sit well with her. Though she wanted to hold off a little longer, the force of her emotion pushed words forth.

"What is in your head?" she finally blurted.

He didn't budge. Just kept staring straight ahead.

"I mean...if you weren't going to let me give him something to think about, why didn't *you*?" she huffed.

Still nothing.

"I just don't understand. You don't agree with David, do you?" She knew her words had an accusing tone. But she couldn't stop herself.

He turned to look at her. "How can you ask that?"

She crossed her arms. "How can *I* ask that? How can you sit by and let him say those things?"

He frowned. "What makes you think I did any such thing?"

"I was there. You discouraged my speaking up, and I didn't hear you give him your two cents, either."

"Not in front of everyone. But I assure you, I did."

Her jaw slackened, and she widened her eyes. "You did?"

"Yes. While you were stewing in the kitchen, cleaning up, I sat him down and told him a few things."

"You did?" She wasn't sure she was ready to forgive him yet, but she was touched by his effort.

"I made sure he had a real good dose of reality."

"But why wouldn't you let me do that?"

"There is no need to shame someone for a difference of opinion. I know you, darling. If you had laid out your thoughts, it would have only raised the temperature of the moment."

"I don't even know what to say to that. I can't believe you don't trust me to be nice."

He arched a brow. "Do you trust yourself to be nice?"

"Well, I—"

"Be honest."

"Okay. I wasn't thinking about holding back."

"And I didn't want you to embarrass our friends and loved ones in your attempt to correct someone. Especially someone like that, who I believed would only get more riled up."

She wanted to bite back, to defend her position. But he was right. She would have lost control of her tongue in a heartbeat. In fact, she almost had.

"Sometimes it's better to keep silent and let someone prove themselves a fool than join them and make yourself out to be one, as well."

Again, she opened her mouth to respond in haste. Then thought better of it. She took some deep breaths and considered his words. He was thinking about her. It hadn't been so much about David's feelings as saving her from making a mistake she would have regretted.

"Thank you," she said, leaning into him.

"That's what I'm here for...to support you and keep you honest. And you do the same for me."

She looped her arms around his bent one and pressed a kiss to the side of his face. "My hero."

His light laugh filled the space around her and warmed her within. Once again, she was thankful for a man who really saw her. And loved her for who she was—rough edges and all.

December

SILVER AND GOLD

Dorothy scanned the great room at the Miller Ranch homestead. Brandon had brought a fine tree in, and Amanda used her unique touch to make it festive. Now, however, she chased Oliver around the room, trying to keep him from the popcorn. The older woman chuckled to herself. That woman's hands were full. But full of good things.

Samuel held Louise next to himself and read her a book—likely a Christmas tale. Maybe that one from Charles Dickens. What was it called? Oh yes, *A Christmas Carol*. Hopefully, it wouldn't frighten the child. Dorothy had heard it had ghosts in it. What kind of joy-filled, peace-bringing Christmas story had ghosts?

Sylvia watched the two young children with rapt attention.

Dorothy turned to Owen who, even then, was putting on his coat and grabbing for hers. How she hated to leave this merriment. But they needed to get home. If they lingered, they would be caught in the dark, facing the chillier ride home.

Owen stepped toward her and held out her coat. She

pushed her arms into the sleeves, thankful for its warmth. Especially as they were about to step outside. It had been dreadfully cold of late. And she couldn't help but wonder if there wasn't something more in the air.

Brandon moved to where she and Owen stood. "Thanks for your help with the decorations."

Cooking and cleaning may be part of her job, but the younger Millers never missed a chance to tell her, or Owen, how they appreciated them. It was heart-warming. And it didn't get old for Dorothy. It was nice to be so loved.

"It was truly our pleasure." Owen spoke for the both of them. She didn't mind one bit. It had been a pleasure.

"You going to get a tree for your place?" Brandon folded his arms over his chest and leaned back into his heels.

She and Owen exchanged a look. It was she who put forth their plan. "We might collect one from behind the barn. We have a couple of prospects there."

Brandon's gaze held hers. She could almost hear his thoughts—*Those trees are so...small. Will they suit the occasion?*

"Besides, we don't have as much room. A smaller tree will do us just fine." She smiled. There was not a chance she would let Owen go hunting down a tree, chop it down, and carry it to the cabin. Not with the way his hip had been since October.

She had threatened Owen within an inch of his life if he dared try it when she was not home. That was her real fear. He so wanted to make every Christmas special.

Brandon nodded and smiled. "Sounds as if you've thought it out."

"Yes. She has," Owen inserted. "She's always thinking ahead."

Jerking her head around toward her husband, she watched for a sign of anything deeper about the jest. Did he not care for her restrictions on him? They were for his own good! His features were relaxed except for the smile that warmed them.

She returned it, glad that he was more settled about the whole thing.

"Shall we?" he held up a hand in the direction of the door.

"Yes." Today had worn on her more than usual. She was ready for her bed all of a sudden.

"Goodnight, then." Brandon stretched a hand toward the door latch.

"See you tomorrow," Dorothy said, gathering the folds of her coat about her, preparing for the rush of chilled air.

It came. But it did so seconds before Brandon reached the door. A forceful puff of air whipped into the room, swirling around those standing at the door.

Eli stomped into the house, dusted in white.

White? Was that...snow?

The ranch hand pulled off his hat, his cheeks red from being slapped by the wind. He nearly bumped into Brandon. "Sorry, boss."

Then he seemed to notice her and Owen.

"So glad I got here in time."

"In time for what? Is it snowing?" Brandon's voice was incredulous.

"In time to catch Cook and Uncle Owen," Eli said. "It's really coming down. I don't think it's a good idea for anyone to go anywhere right now."

"But if we don't go now," Dorothy thought out loud, "we won't be able to get home before dark."

Gentle hands landed on her arm. It was Amanda. "That won't be a problem. You can have our room."

"Nonsense. Samuel and Louise have already given up their rooms to Sylvia and David."

Amanda gave her a hard look. "We can make a pallet on the floor in Oliver's room for Brandon and me."

Dorothy opened her mouth to protest, but Amanda cut her off.

"I won't hear it, Cook. You need your rest."

"So do you." The fight in her was weak, and her statement betrayed that. It was unlikely Owen could get back upright after a night on the floor. Not now.

Amanda smiled. "We'll be fine. Besides, we've been in Oliver's room so much lately, it'll be a relief to not have to walk so far to put him back to bed."

That probably was true. Now that the little boy was mobile and even more active, it did seem rather impossible to contain him. But Dorothy hadn't considered that the same was true at night.

"Ma," came a strong voice from behind Amanda. And, as she stepped to the side to turn, Dorothy spotted Samuel standing there, with wide eyes and a big grin. "Can we go play in the snow?"

He appeared much younger in that moment. Like a little child again.

"Sorry." Amanda shook her head. "It might get worse, and I need you all to stay inside until we see what will become of it."

Samuel's face fell.

Owen set a hand on his shoulder. "It'll be there in the morning. I'm sure of it."

"You think so?" The hopeful gaze returned.

Brandon nodded. "Sure. I bet you'll have at least a couple of days to enjoy it."

Samuel nodded.

"You gonna finish telling me about the ghost of Christmas present?" Louise called from the corner of the room. Her eyes were as wide as his had been.

Ghost of Christmas present? Gracious! What a strange story indeed.

Samuel moved back to where he had left Louise, snuggled her next to him once more, and resumed reading.

Dorothy looked to Owen, still uncertain about the prospect of staying. He leaned in as Brandon lifted the small bundle of young Oliver and tugged Amanda over to the fireplace. "We should be thankful we weren't out in it already."

That was true. They could have gotten caught out there. Images of a broken or stuck wagon wheel filled her mind, and she was even more thankful.

Owen pulled off his coat and reached for hers. "No sense in that thing now."

She let him help her slip it off.

Amanda waved her over. Before long, she and Owen were settled on the sofa, listening to Samuel, whether they wanted to or not.

The family was settled in the great room while the snowstorm continued to buffet the windows. It was quite a sight. Not one that they got all that often.

David had even joined them after disappearing to his temporary room for a while. As usual, Dorothy bristled at his manner. His superior attitude was always evident in the way he held himself, looked around himself, or how he regarded others. It was quite off-putting.

But that was not what she wanted to focus on. Louise had fallen asleep, and Samuel put the book down. He said he'd finish it tomorrow. The story had intrigued Dorothy, and she wondered about the earlier portion that she hadn't heard. The question was whether she was interested enough to actually read it.

The time around the fireplace had been pleasant. And the

family had become quiet some time ago, just enjoying the fire and its warmth. It was nice.

"This year is coming to a close rather quickly," Brandon said, looking around the room. "Only a little over a week remaining."

That was true. But what was he getting at? Other than stating the obvious? Everyone watched him.

"God has been good this year. The cattle drive went off without a hitch. We brought in a good amount of money. Cutie and Mariena are back in Wharton City for good. Dan and Lily added a little boy to their household. Slim and Ada got married. So many wonderful things!"

That was true. This had been a big year for the Miller family and friends.

"I wonder what each of you would say has been the best part of this year." Brandon's gaze moved from person to person.

It made Dorothy uncomfortable. These types of prying questions always did. Why did he have to go and get all mushy?

Owen pulled her closer with his arm that was already around her shoulders.

"I have to say that I'm glad Oliver started sleeping through the night," Amanda said on a sigh. "And I can get some good sleep. Well, until he started getting up again."

Brandon kissed her forehead. "It'll go back to normal soon."

She closed her eyes and rested against him.

Samuel piped up. "I'm glad for the snow!"

"The answer is still 'no,' son," Brandon said with a laugh. "Tomorrow."

Samuel fell against the back of the chair. The movement caused Louise to stir. She snuggled into the arm of the chair a bit more and continued sleeping.

Sylvia's voice broke into the silence created by everyone's focus on Louise. "I haven't had much to be grateful for these last years. They have been hard. Harder than I imagined. But I gained a son-in-law, who loves my daughter and makes her so happy. And I get to spend the holiday with my grandchildren. My heart is full."

The tenderness in Sylvia's comment squeezed Dorothy's heart. Losing her betrothed so many years ago had been unimaginably painful. What would it be like to lose a husband? That nearly stole the breath from her—the thought of being without Owen. She prayed she'd never know it.

"There have been so many things this year to be glad for. But none more than my Dorothy," Owen said, rubbing her shoulder. "She is my best friend, and I can't believe I waited so long to tell her I was sweet on her."

"Neither can we," Brandon added.

Dorothy's cheeks heated. Her Owen was so good to her.

David leaned forward. "If I had to choose something, it would be my father's bestowing on me a partnership in his law firm."

Why wasn't she surprised? If anyone could, he would find a way to compliment himself with his gratitude.

The room became quiet again. Dorothy leaned into her husband and watched the flames lapping at the air in the hearth.

"What about you, Cook?"

Dorothy looked up.

It was Amanda who had spoken. And her gaze settled on Dorothy.

Dorothy sighed. "That is difficult. I have had such a good year. And Owen has made everything all the more special... being with me every day, making me a better woman with his kindness and care."

Amanda nodded before turning her attention to her own husband.

Owen squeezed Dorothy's hand as they all fell into a comfortable silence once again and Dorothy continued to reflect on the year. Through all the ups and downs, she had truly been thankful to have Owen by her side.

Later that evening, Dorothy slid into the bed provided. It was strange, being in her day clothes. But the chill in the air had her pulling the blanket as high as she could and still poke her nose out.

"Cold?" Owen asked.

"Did my chattering teeth give me away?"

He chuckled.

She liked the warm sound that emitted from him when he stifled a laugh like that. It vibrated in his chest and seemed to brighten the space all around him. Truly, she was a lucky woman to have his heart.

"You know," he said as he scooted a little closer, "I've been thinking."

"That's dangerous."

"Yes, but I have been, all the same."

She closed her eyes. Sleep would come for her quickly tonight. After a few moments, she realized he had not continued. "Were you planning to share these thoughts?"

"Just making sure you're paying attention. It's one of my better ponderings. I don't want to waste it." His grin was evident in the way his voice sounded.

"I'm awake." She resisted the urge to poke him.

"We have had a good year."

"Um hmm," she mumbled. The urge to slip into the calm, quiet recesses of sleep was becoming more compelling.

"I think we have learned better how to share. And be honest."

There was truth to his words. It hadn't always been easy, but the things they faced had brought them closer.

"You know what the Bible says—'a wife of good character, who can find? Her worth is more than that of rubies. Her husband has confidence in her and lacks nothing'."

That was what the Proverbs said. She had always read it and dreamed that one day she would be that kind of wife. Then, as the years went by, she prayed that she would at least have the chance to love and be loved in the bonds of matrimony. And she had not thought much more about her actual value as a wife. These words were rather challenging.

"You are such a woman," Owen said softly, as if he could sense her thoughts. "You are the greatest treasure I have or could ask for."

"Oh, you old coot. You sure are sweet." She bit her lip then. His love for her was plain to see. But it wasn't often she thought about whether he valued her in such a way. Now, she knew.

"And just as surely, you are a blessing to me, Dorothy Miller."

She leaned into him, laying her head on his shoulder. "I never knew I could be this happy."

"You deserve it, my dear."

"Do I?" That didn't seem right. Was it wrong to declare that one deserved such good things?

"In Christ, my darling, you are deserving of every good thing."

A wave of peace overcame her. Yes. This was truth. And this was God's love for her—that he gave her Owen and gave her to him.

For all the years of their lives.

Keep reading for a preview of the next book in the Convenient Risk Series!

Thank you, dear reader, for for reading along with me! If you enjoyed this story, I would sincerely appreciate if you would submit a review. It would mean so much to me!

To read more about these characters, follow along with the Convenient Risk Series. Find it at:
https://saraturnquist.com/convenient-risk-series/

A Sneak Peek

A LESS CONVENIENT ARRANGEMENT

The world had lost its sheen. Its vibrancy. Its life.

Sadie Rose Perkins stared at the ceiling and was dreading yet another day. How could she face the people of Wharton City with their accusations and stares? How could she face her life?

Couldn't she just turn over and let sleep claim her once more? Perhaps permanently? Nothing about this was fair. Perhaps. Did she have this coming?

How had she not seen it? She should have.

Had it only been a week since she woke to find her father gone? As if that hadn't been heartbreaking enough, the following days brought with them an even greater distress—the revelation that the man she had trusted, the town's once prominent and respected banker, had embezzled from the bank. Really, from the good people of this town.

He had betrayed everyone. Everyone. Even her. Yes, she should have noticed that something was off. Somehow.

Would the townsfolk ever forgive her? How could they?

Perhaps she deserved as much. She should have seen the signs.

Father had been more distant, absorbed with matters of the bank.

And he had been home less and less. Even then, he often closed himself in his study.

How had she not seen? Not suspected?

Yes, she had earned blame in this.

If only she could apologize enough. But no one would hear it. Scowls and narrowed gazes were the common greeting now. And would continue to be.

Sadie covered her face. What was the point?

Outside her open bedroom door, movement in the great room drew her attention. Mother.

The woman had been agitated. Even more so than usual. This whole situation had indeed taken its toll on the older woman. If only Sadie could shield her mother. From the burden. From the shame.

Sliding her feet from what little warmth the covers offered, Sadie shivered. Still, she forced herself to sit and press her vulnerable soles to the cold wood. A chill shot through her—right up her spine. But she had to push on. Mother needed her.

She grabbed her knit shawl, a precious gift that reminded Sadie of a time when her mother was more capable, and pulled it around her shoulders. While it did nothing for her cold feet, perhaps it would keep her upper body from freezing. Padding into the great room, she found her mother by a shelf. As she watched, the woman lifted a book, flipped through the pages, and tossed the volume to the floor, only to pick up another from its perch.

"Mother? What's the matter?" Sadie crossed the room and set a hand to her mother's arm.

The woman turned a hollow gaze on Sadie. "I...can't seem to find your father."

Sadie's heart dropped. Not this again.

Shifting her focus back to her task, her mother said, "I know he left a map. I just can't find it." Her hands shook as she poured over the next book.

Reaching for the hands that had done much to comfort her over the years, Sadie attempted to still the tremors. Mother's fingers were as ice. How long had she been up and about? Sadie lifted the book from her mother's reach.

It seemed at first that Mother would protest. She opened her mouth, and her lips moved as if she spoke, but no sound came forth.

"You must be cold." Sadie tugged at the older woman.

Mother stood her ground, but her gaze set on Sadie once more. If only the stare wasn't so vacant.

Sadie's heart squeezed.

Then there was a spark in Mother's eyes. "Shouldn't you be getting ready for school?"

Sadie frowned. She never quite knew what to do in these moments. They had become more frequent of late. Since Father's flight in the night, Mother had been in a constant state of confusion it seemed.

"Mother, I finished school. Two years ago."

The woman's graying hair was tangled. Sadie would have to do something about that. And her thin, frayed nightgown needed attention.

Deep brown eyes looked about Sadie's features. Did she try to discern the truth? Could she? "School is over? Then I should get supper on the table."

Mother pulled free. Then she walked across the cluttered area, stumbling over the pile of books, and moved toward her bedroom.

Sadie paused, taking in a deep breath and releasing it. Then she followed.

Her mother stood in front of an open wardrobe. "Now where are the potatoes?"

"In the kitchen." Sadie could not help the moisture building behind her eyes. "Mother, let me help you get something warmer on…"

"I can't seem to find the potatoes." She whirled toward Sadie, that empty look about her again.

Time to try a different tactic. One that usually worked. But Sadie regretted resorting to it. She just couldn't do this. Not right now. Hadn't she earned a moment of peace? Just for a minute? "Mother, we had supper."

"Oh?" The woman's confusion intensified. As did Sadie's distress.

"Yes," Sadie forced her voice to stay calm. "It's time to lay down."

Mother's gaze slid to the window. "It's so bright."

"Yes, it is. But it will be dark soon." She laid gentle hands on Mother's shoulders and prodded her in the direction of the bed. "You have a big day tomorrow, and you need your sleep."

"What about your father?" Even as she protested, Mother sat on the edge of the mattress. "I need to—"

"I'll take care of Father. You rest."

Though there wasn't so much as a hint of certainty in Mother's eyes, the woman lay down and let Sadie pull the covers to her chin.

"Just for a minute."

"All right, Ma, just for a minute."

Then the woman closed her eyes.

Sadie tiptoed across the floor as quietly as possible so that she was in the hall before she fell apart. She shoved her fist against her mouth to muffle her sobs as she sank to the floor.

To read more, find *A Less Convenient Arrangement* here:

https://saraturnquist.com/a-less-convenient-arrangement/

A Less Convenient Path (Book 3)

She is in a hopeless situation. He doesn't have a chance.

Mariena's native nation has been ordered to a Reservation but her tribe was attacked en route. She and her young brother wander in a wilderness filled with dangerous animals. Until...

Cutie happens upon them as he flees his own demons. Can Mariena awaken something he never expected? Even bring him to believe in himself once more?

A story of two people without peace. Will they find in each other the very things they are missing?

A Convenient Escape (Book 4)

She has nowhere to go. He has nothing to lose.

Lily has known hardship and rejection. Her brother takes a job at the Miller ranch. Now with no ally, she becomes desperate to get away...by any means necessary.

Dan is prepared to do whatever it takes to ensure Lily is cared for... even if that means proposing marriage.

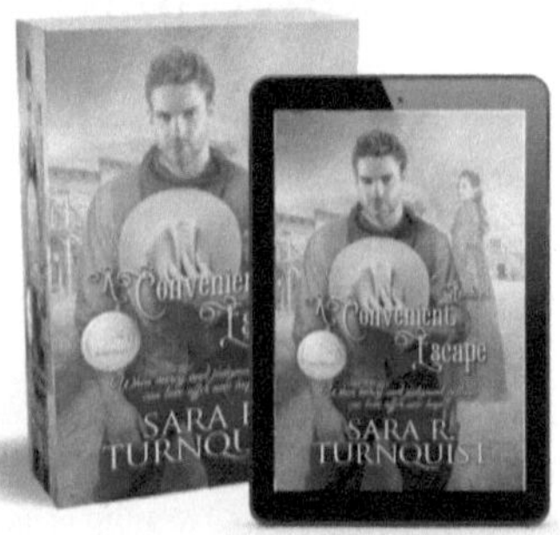

Will they make it to the church? Or find themselves victims of lies, disillusionment, or the ire of an Apache rebel?

An Inconvenient Acquaintance (Book 5)

She wants adventure. He needs a place to belong.

Ada the new schoolteacher in Tombstone. Her desire for independence stems from tales of the west. But she never expected to find herself torn between two men—one who promises safety and security, the other's future is uncertain and offers excitement.

Slim is determined that he will not become involved with a woman of privilege, Ada's fiery personality intrigues him. And soon he is vying for her heart with a man he'd rather not trifle with.

Will they find what they seek in each other? Or will they become caught up in a shootout at the O.K. Corral?

These Golden Years (Book 6)

A collection of short stories through the year.

Dorothy "Cook" Miller and "Uncle" Owen Miller are living their best life and marriage. Though it is not without bumps along the way. Join them as they walk through the year together with its measure of mishaps and laughs. This collection of short stories shows that marriage can be fraught with misunderstanding. But also has its share of lighter moments.

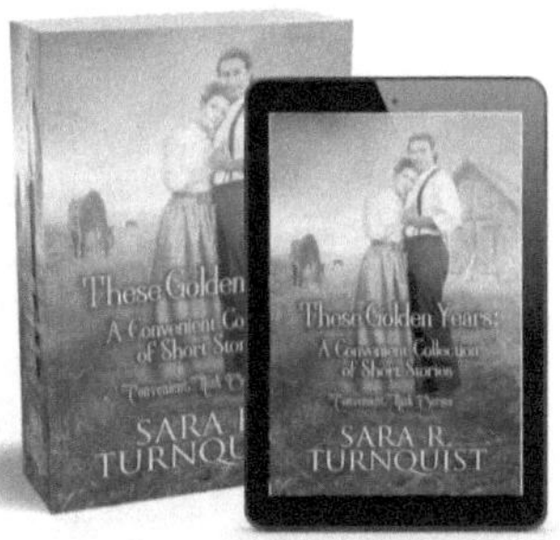

An Less Convenient Arrangement (Book 7)

She has lost all hope. He has little desire to stay by her side.

Sadie finds herself in dire straits after her father absconds with everyone's money. Her mother's failing mental stability also becomes a trial she is not certain she can overcome. Is there anywhere she can turn?

Though his one goal is to return to Richmond and a partnership in his father's law firm, David is drawn to Sadie and softens to her plight. He offers what help he can, but resists being pulled into the mess that has become her life. Until he starts to care beyond that initial attraction.

Can she stand strong against the challenges facing her?
Will David risk following his heart regardless of the cost?
Or take the first out offered to him?

Ranch Hands Collection

Four Stories from the Miller Ranch

Acknowledgments

Thank you so much to everyone who has read or listened to the book along the way. You have been a part of this work in a real way. Also for those who weathered my writer-ness throughout this process.

This book was an idea born from a conversation with a dear friend, Mary Wood. So she deserves a good bit of credit for the existance of this collection in the first place.

I have to acknowledge the input of my craft partner, Kelly Hollman, who continues to read and hear my work, offering priceless feedback and critique.

Cindy Smith, you are always ready and willing to offer immediate gratification to this writer when you look at the scenes under construction. Not to dismiss that the plotting sessions have made this book what it is. A thank youd does not feel adequate.

Word Weavers Page 32, you ladies have given me such encouragement and wonderful advice. Thank you.

Hannah Conway, my writing mentor, who is part of every book through advice and letting me bounce ideas off her. You are an inspiration to me...and I hope I can be one millionth the assistance for you one day.

My editor, Julie Sherwood, I don't know how I would be where I am as a writer without you kicking my butt and keeping me honest each and every novel. Keep it real. Every. Time.

Cora Graphics, I continue to be amazed by your gifts with graphic design. My books shine because of your covers.

VerBull Photography, thanks for getting my "good side" :-)

My husband and number one fan, Greg Turnquist, this quarantine has been nuts, but you still made time for the writing to happen. You are it, babe. We're doing it.

For my sister, you make me want to be better. For my dad, you make me feel so good to have achieved this dream of writing. For my mom, I will love you forever. And for my kids, you keep me inspired.

Last, but certainly not least, my readers, you give me a reason to keep writing.

About the Author

Sara is a coffee lovin', word slinging, Historical Romance author whose super power is converting caffeine into novels. She loves those odd little tidbits of history that are stranger than fiction. That's what inspires her. Well, that and a good love story.

But of all the love stories she knows, hers is her favorite. She lives happily with her own Prince Charming and their gaggle of minions. Three to be exact. They sure know how to distract a writer! But, alas, the stories must be written, even if it must happen in the wee hours of the morning.

Sara is an avid reader and enjoys reading and writing clean Historical Romance when she's not traveling.

Please follow along with her journey through her newsletter at: http://saraturnquist.com/list

Happy Reading!

facebook.com/AuthorSaraRTurnquist

instagram.com/sararturnquist

x.com/sararturnquist

youtube.com/@SaraRTurnquist

pinterest.com/sararturnquist

Also by Sara R. Turnquist

CONVENIENT RISK SERIES

A Convenient Risk

An Inconvenient Christmas

A Less Convenient Path

A Convenient Escape

An Inconvenient Acquaintance

These Golden Years

A Less Convenient Arrangement

Ranch Hands Collection (ebook only)

CRIPPLE CREEK SERIES

Hope in Cripple Creek

Christmas in Cripple Creek

Faith in Cripple Creek

Love in Cripple Creek

~Prequels~

Leaving Waverly

Leaving Stoneybrook

LADY OF BOHEMIA SERIES

The Lady Bornekova

The Lady and the Hussites

The Lady and Her Champion

The Lady and Her Secret

RAILWAY ROMANCE SERIES

Laura, The Tycoon's Daughter

ACROSS THE YEARS SERIES

Among the Pages

Between the Lines

STANDALONE NOVELS

The General's Wife

Trail of Fears

Off to War